THE SECRET AGENT ON FLIGHT 101

Rarely do magicians reveal their professional secrets. Consequently Frank and Joe Hardy are amazed when a well-known magician, the Incredible Hexton, offers to reveal the secret of his "Vanishing Man Act" and invites Mr. Hardy to be the subject. When their detective father fails to reappear, his sons are convinced that something sinister is afoot, despite Hexton's insistence that Mr. Hardy is playing a joke on them.

While desperately searching for their father, Frank and Joe find themselves working with SKOOL, a U.S. organization of crack secret agents pitted against UGLI, an international ring of spies stealing government secrets from the U.S. and other democratic countries.

In a lighthouse off the coast of New England and in Scotland, Frank and Joe and their pal Chet Morton grimly match wits with UGLI's evil agents. With cool daring the three boys invade the magician's Scottish castle, where an astounding surprise awaits them.

The young detectives' gripping adventures culminate in a dramatic climax when they unmask the secret agent on Flight 101.

"Good luck, lad!" the pilot called

The Hardy Boys Mystery Stories®

THE SECRET AGENT ON FLIGHT 101

BY

FRANKLIN W. DIXON

GROSSET & DUNLAP
Publishers • New York
A member of The Putnam & Grosset Group

PRINTED ON RECYCLED PAPER

CONTENTS

THE SECRET
AGENT
ON
FLIGHT 101

CHAPTER I

A Vanishing Act

"How can the hand be quicker than the eye?" asked Chet Morton. "That's hard to believe!" He climbed into the back seat of the Hardy boys' convertible next to Joe.

"Perhaps the Incredible Hexton will convince you," remarked Frank, who was at the wheel. "All set, Dad?" he asked the handsome man beside him.

"Take off!" Mr. Hardy said, smiling.

It was Friday evening. Bayport High had closed for summer vacation the day before. To celebrate, the Hardy boys and their stout friend Chet were being treated to a magician's show in the nearby city of Claymore.

"I read in a newspaper," Chet went on, "how pickpockets use sleight-of-hand methods. In fact, I have the clipping here in my—" Suddenly he sat bolt upright. "My wallet!" he cried. "It's gone!"

Frank brought the car to a stop. "Are you sure?" he asked.

Chet searched his pockets frantically. "It's gone all right!"

"Probably dropped out when you got into the car," Frank suggested.

"Then we'd better go back," Mr. Hardy said.

Joe tried to hide a grin. But Chet noticed it. "Wait a minute!" He eyed Joe suspiciously. "Okay, mastermind. Hand it over!"

Joe burst out laughing and gave his chum a brown leather wallet. "Just wanted to prove to you the hand really is quicker than the eye."

"You caught me off guard," Chet replied good-naturedly.

Joe Hardy, blond and seventeen, enjoyed joking and was more impulsive than his dark-haired, eighteen-year-old brother. Both boys were trim all-around athletes. Chet, their schoolmate, had a chunky build and played on the Bayport High football team.

"Let's go, boys!" said Fenton Hardy, grinning. "Any more pocket-picking and I'll pull you in!"

Frank and Joe's father was a nationally known detective who had earned his fame as a member of the New York City Police Department. After his retirement from the force, he had set up his own sleuthing organization. Both sons were following in his footsteps and already had solved many challenging mysteries on their own. Chet often joined in their adventures. Although the stout boy preferred safer pursuits, no danger could make him desert his friends.

"What do you know about Hexton the magician?" Frank asked his father.

Mr. Hardy said the man was a performer of some renown throughout the world, and was much acclaimed for his demonstrations of sleight of hand.

Joe asked, "Dad, do you by any chance have a professional interest in him?"

The detective laughed but did not reply and Joe decided not to press his query further. But he sensed that he had hit upon the truth.

They drove into Claymore, parked in the lot behind the theater, and took their seats just as the houselights dimmed. A tall, dark figure slipped through the curtains and the spotlight blazed upon the Incredible Hexton.

The gaunt magician wore a top hat, flowing black cape, and carried a silver-handled cane. His face sent a chill through Chet.

Hexton had heavy brows, a sharply pointed chin, and the piercing eyes of a medieval sorcerer. He moved into his performance with a cat-like grace which indicated a disciplined and powerful body.

The boys watched eagerly as the magician caused coins, cards, and other small objects to disappear, then reappear at his fingertips.

The finale of the show was billed as the "Vanishing Man Act." Hexton led a short, muscular aide to a boxlike compartment, walled in on three sides by curtains and on the front by draperies. He opened and closed these a couple of times. Inside the curtained area was what looked like an oversized picture frame, supported at each end by posts.

Hexton's aide was strapped to a plank, which the magician and a tall, thin assistant set horizontally into the frame. This was tilted toward the audience at a forty-five-degree angle.

Hexton closed the small curtain and gestured with his cane. In seconds the curtain was reopened. The audience gasped in amazement! The magician's aide, and the plank to which he had been strapped, had vanished!

Hexton bowed low, and his aide strolled onto the stage from the wings, to thunderous applause from the audience. Hexton bowed several times more, and stepped behind the curtain.

"Great performance!" Frank said as he rose from his seat and stretched.

"Do you know how he did it, Dad?" Joe asked.

"I have an idea. Let's go backstage. I think it would be interesting to talk to Hexton."

The detective and his three companions made their way to a door at the side of the stage. They went through it and up a short flight of steps to the wing, where they found Hexton.

Mr. Hardy introduced himself and his party. "You had us baffled," he said. "Good show!"

"Especially the last trick," said Joe. "That was great!"

The performer smiled cordially. "Perhaps you would like to see how it is done."

Frank looked surprised. "I thought magicians never gave away their secrets."

"Customarily they don't," Hexton replied smoothly, "but, you see, I have recognized your name. I know Fenton Hardy is a star performer in his own field. We both deal in secrets. Mr. Hardy, my job is to mystify, yours just the opposite. I will show you the trick as a professional courtesy."

"That's very gracious of you," the detective replied.

"Not at all," Hexton said quickly. "I have a feeling we ought to become better acquainted."

Mr. Hardy smiled. "An excellent idea."

"One moment," said Hexton. "I must alert my assistant. In the meantime, will you boys please take seats down in the auditorium." Hexton strode off but returned in a couple of minutes. "Follow me, Mr. Hardy."

He led the detective onstage in the now-empty theater. "Would you do me the honor of being my subject?" he asked with a sweeping bow.

The short assistant strapped Fenton Hardy to the plank. With the three boys watching intently, the magician closed the curtain and waved his cane. When he opened the compartment, the subject had vanished.

"That's neat!" Chet said.

The boys watched for Mr. Hardy to reappear. When some time went by and he did not come out of the wings, Frank and Joe became worried.

"What's happened?" Frank asked anxiously. He and Joe ran onto the stage to examine the compartment, but Hexton blocked them.

"I can't permit you to inspect my device," he said, dropping his pleasant manner.

"Then tell us where our father is!" Joe demanded.

"I don't know," Hexton said slyly. "He must be playing some kind of joke on you."

Joe moved toward the magician. "Step aside. We're going to take a look at that gadget of yours."

Hexton called quickly, "Vordo! Stony!"

Two men emerged from the wings. The first one appeared to be nearly seven feet tall. His massive shoulders, muscular arms, and hard features made him a formidable sight. The other was the thin fellow who had helped with the vanishing act.

"See to it that these boys leave immediately," the magician ordered.

Joe was ready to fight, but Frank caught his brother's upraised arm. Perhaps Hexton was telling the truth.

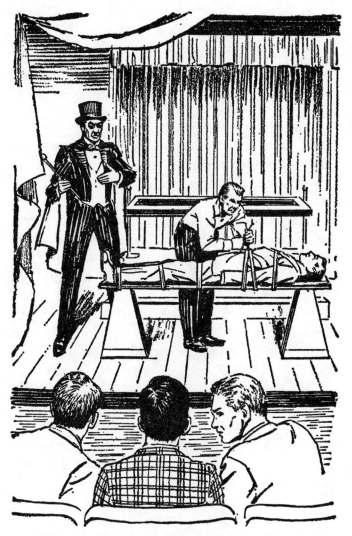

The assistant strapped Mr. Hardy to the plank

Joe acceded. "All right, have it your way!" he said. "But we'll be back!"

The trio hurried out of the theater. Joe insisted upon going to nearby Claymore Police Headquarters to request that a couple of officers go back to investigate.

"All right," said Frank.

When the group returned to the theater, Hexton became enraged. "If you try to look at my equipment without a warrant, I'll sue you!" he stormed.

The officer told the boys that since there was no evidence of a crime, the only thing they could do was to file a missing-persons report.

"But we can't just sit around and wait!" Joe declared hotly.

"On the other hand, it's possible Dad is staying away on purpose," Frank reasoned in a low tone. "Let's wait a while before we report him missing."

Joe was not satisfied. "At least let's search the theater."

The police agreed to this and the manager was summoned. He gave permission, but stressed the point that he had no jurisdiction over Hexton's equipment.

The magician and his assistants glared at the Hardys and Chet as they inspected the stage thoroughly. Then they searched other sections of the theater. There was no sign of Fenton Hardy.

Frank suggested that they return home, in the hope that his father would try to reach them there.

Deeply worried, the three boys hurried across the dark parking lot and got into the Hardy car. As they sped along a straight stretch of road leading from the city, Chet looked out the rear window. He noticed the headlights of a pickup truck drawing swiftly closer.

"Some character is tailgating us," Chet said. "Doesn't he know that's dangerous?"

"Best thing is to let him go by," Frank replied, and pulled closer to the shoulder of the road.

The small truck roared past the Hardys' car.

"A speed demon!" Joe said sarcastically as the truck disappeared from sight.

The route Frank had chosen led them along a narrow, winding mountain road, bordered on one side by a guard rail. Below it was a sheer drop of several hundred feet.

As the car rounded a sharp curve, the boys were horror-stricken to see the headlights of a car directly in front of them. They had only the fraction of a second to brace themselves for a collision!

CHAPTER II

The Hexton File

CRASH! There was a loud, piercing sound of shattering glass as the oncoming headlights made contact. Yet there was no collision! Like an apparition, the other vehicle had vanished completely.

Frank struggled to maneuver the car away from the guard rail. He jammed on the brakes and skidded to a stop. They all looked startled.

"Wh-what happened?" Chet asked.

"I don't know," Frank said. "This is weird—"

Joe pulled out a flashlight. "Let's go back up the road and investigate!"

The boys walked to where they had encountered the headlights. As Joe played the beam along the road, they noticed broken glass scattered about. Frank picked up a fragment.

"Look at this!" he said.

"It's a piece of mirror!" exclaimed Chet.

"So that's it!" Frank exploded. "Someone set

a mirror on the road. What we saw was the reflection of our own headlights!"

Joe's eyes widened in anger. "We might have swerved over the embankment!"

"Exactly!" Frank answered. "Whoever planted the glass put it too close to the bend in the road. We came upon it so quickly I didn't have time to swerve!"

The young sleuths wondered if Hexton or his assistants had set the trap for them. Or had it been intended for another unsuspecting victim?

"This mystery is getting too dangerous," Chet said gravely. "A guy could get hurt."

"Don't worry. We'll get to the bottom of it," Frank vowed.

The Hardys searched the area more closely. Joe picked up a sliver of wood. He noticed several similar pieces scattered along the road.

"What do you make of this?" he asked.

Frank examined it. "Undoubtedly this is part of a wooden easel that was used to support the mirror."

"Magicians often use them in their acts," remarked Joe. "Hexton could have had a big mirror brought here in a pickup truck."

Frank agreed. "The one that passed us was certainly traveling fast enough to reach this spot well ahead of us."

"If Hexton did plant the mirror, how could he know we'd take this road?" Chet inquired.

"It's the fastest way back to Bayport," Frank replied. "He may have had us followed."

After scuffing the glass and wood off the road, the boys drove on. At the Morton farm on the outskirts of Bayport, Chet got out.

"S'long, fellows," he said. "Keep me posted about your dad."

Frank and Joe drove home in silence. Their mother and Aunt Gertrude were waiting for them in the living room. Reluctantly the boys told what had happened.

"Oh dear!" their aunt shrilled. "Quick! Call the police. Fenton's been kidnapped!"

Gertrude Hardy, tall and angular, was the sister of Fenton Hardy. Although she admired the sleuthing abilities of her brother and nephews, she constantly worried about the dangers involved.

Mrs. Hardy, an attractive and gracious woman, was too stunned by the shock of her husband's disappearance to talk. Frank put a comforting arm about her.

"In case Dad disappeared on purpose, let's not notify the police. Joe and I will find him. He may not be far away."

The boys excused themselves, then went to their father's study.

"I think Aunty's right about the kidnapping," said Joe. "Dad must have had something pretty big on Hexton."

"In that case," Frank said, "we ought to find it in his files."

But there was no record of Hexton under the letter H.

"Try M for magician," Joe suggested.

Frank looked. "Not there."

They checked several other headings, but did not find any mention of the man. Then Joe noticed a folder marked "School."

"That's funny," he said. "I don't remember Dad having a case to do with a school."

He took out the file and opened it. "Frank! Look here! This is it!"

Fascinated, the boys read the notes. Mr. Hardy described the magician as a diabolical man who for years had headed a gang of thieves. Working as the crew for his show, they moved about the country with him, pulling the robberies he planned. The detective had discovered the setup recently. "So far no real evidence," he had noted. Written at the bottom of the page was: "Last two years agent UGLI."

"UGLI!" Joe exclaimed. "Undercover Global League of Informants!"

Frank gave a low whistle. "This is really big! UGLI is the most powerful espionage ring in the world."

"And hostile to democratic countries," added Joe.

The boys exchanged grim looks. If their father

had been kidnapped, he was in ruthless hands!

"I think I know now why this is filed under school," said Frank.

Joe nodded. "That's probably a camouflage word for SKOOL. Dad must be working for them."

Both boys had heard of the famous supranational counterespionage ring which worked on behalf of democratic powers. The letters stood for Secret Knowledge Of Organized Lawbreakers.

"If only we could contact them," said Frank, "they might be able to give us a lead. But the organization is so secret, there's no way to reach them."

"Unless they've called you first," said Joe. "Maybe Dad left a note on how to get in touch."

But a thorough search turned up no information. The boys perused the report again and learned that for the past two years State Department secrets had been leaking out of Washington to enemy countries at an increasing rate. The detective had written, "Offices, cars, and homes of diplomatic corps must be very cleverly bugged. Agents probably transmit microtape to couriers who take it abroad."

On the margin at the left were the words, "See Dell."

Frank and Joe searched the file and all the other drawers in the room, but could find no further reference to Dell. Who was he?

Before they put the Hexton report away, Frank read aloud the note at the end of it: " 'Do not think Hexton is aware of investigation. Perhaps should discuss with Frank and Joe when more substantial evidence is found.' "

"It's dated yesterday!" Joe exclaimed.

"Somehow Hexton must have learned that Dad was onto his game," Frank observed.

"And our showing up at the theater," Joe said, "probably made him nervous. So he pulled a kidnapping."

Frank reminded Joe of the magician's suggestion that the two men get better acquainted. "I'll bet Dad thought if he went along with the idea he might be able to get the goods on Hexton. The first step was taking part in the trick."

"But what a risk!" said Joe.

"You know Dad," Frank said quietly. "If he figured it was worth while, he'd take it."

The night wore on with no word. Finally Aunt Gertrude insisted upon phoning a missing-persons report to the Bayport police. The next morning there was still no word from the detective, and the police had found nothing.

Frank and Joe decided to drive back to Claymore. They arrived at the theater to find the front door locked. Walking around to the back, they were confronted by a guard. He told them that Hexton had given his last performance the night before and had already departed. The magician had left two of his assistants behind to supervise the packing of the show's equipment.

"Our father disappeared here last evening," Frank said. "We'd like to have a look inside."

"Sorry," the guard answered, "I can't permit anyone in the theater. Manager's orders."

"Then we'd like to see him," Joe said.

"He's not here. I'd advise you to go."

"Okay," Frank signaled Joe with his eyes and the two walked off briskly around the side of the building. There they stopped abruptly and Frank peered back.

After a few minutes the guard left his post and disappeared around the far corner.

"Let's go!" Frank commanded.

Quietly the boys edged their way toward the stage door. They pulled it open and darted inside, stopping to let their eyes adjust to the dim light. Then, cautiously, they made their way to the stage. Nobody was around.

"Where are Hexton's men?" Joe whispered.

"Out for a coffee break," Frank guessed.

The stage was cluttered with packing cases containing the magician's equipment. At the rear the boys spotted the vanishing-man device. It had already been partially dismantled.

"Look! The plank's missing," Joe said. "Maybe packed in one of these cases."

Further examination of the device revealed

that it had a false bottom, beneath which was a secret compartment.

A soft rustling noise had sounded overhead. "What's that?" Frank said. He glanced up in time to see a ballast sandbag hurtling down toward them from the flies.

"Look out!" Frank shouted. He leaped aside, pulling Joe with him. The sandbag crashed to the stage and burst open. The boys looked up and saw a man running along a catwalk.

"After him!" Joe yelled.

"Hold it!" commanded a harsh voice. "Stay right where you are!"

CHAPTER III

The SKOOL Man

THE Hardys whirled to see the theater guard approaching. "So it's you two!" he shouted angrily. "Didn't I tell you to shove off?"

"Yes, but—" Joe began.

"That crash—" the guard cut in. "What happened?" He looked at the sand scattered about the stage.

"Someone tried to drop a sandbag on us," Frank explained.

"A likely story." The guard eyed the boys suspiciously. "You're probably up to something. I'm calling the police!"

Keeping an eye on the boys, the guard walked to a wall telephone and dialed. Within minutes an officer arrived.

"Oh, the Hardy brothers," he said, and turned to the guard. "I heard about these kids. They're trying to find their father."

"I thought that was a gag," the man replied.

"No. It's on the up and up."

The guard apologized and helped the young sleuths examine the sandbag. They discovered that the ropes which held it had been cut.

At that moment the magician's thin assistant walked onstage. When the policeman questioned him, he gave his name as Stony Bleeker. The man said he had been out for a walk and insisted he had had nothing to do with dropping the sandbag.

"Where's the other man who was helping you pack?" Frank asked.

"How should I know?"

"I suppose you're going to tell us that you don't know what happened to our father, either!" Joe said.

"You're nuts!" Bleeker growled.

The Hardys climbed up to examine the flies, but there was no trace of their attacker. "He must have sneaked down the ladder and out the side door while we were hassling with the guard," said Joe.

Back on the stage, the boys found further questioning fruitless. The policeman said he would request that the detective squad investigate the matter.

Stony Bleeker quickly set about packing the rest of Hexton's equipment, telling the policeman that a truck would call for it shortly.

"Well, that's that!" Frank said glumly. "Come on, Joe. Let's go home."

On the way back to Bayport, the boys decided to search their father's study again.

"Maybe we can find out who or what Dell is," Frank said. "That might give us a lead."

But their efforts were of no avail until Frank examined the books on his father's desk. A torn envelope flap was sticking to the back cover of one. On it was the notation, "Kenneth Dell, Great Circle Airways, Westboro, 789-1010."

"You found it!" Joe exclaimed.

The boys surmised that their father had put the book down on the gummed paper and failed to notice later that it had stuck to the cover.

Quickly Frank dialed the Westboro number. A man with a deep, commanding voice answered and identified himself as Kenneth Dell. Frank explained why he had called, and Dell revealed that he was chief of security for Great Circle Airways.

Amazed to hear about the disappearance of Mr. Hardy, Dell said it was imperative that he talk to the young detectives and he would fly to Bayport the following day.

"Meet me outside the airport restaurant at twelve-thirty," Dell said. "I don't want to come to your home for fear we're being watched by Hexton's men. I'll explain everything when I see you."

After church the next day, Frank and Joe drove through the heavy Sunday traffic to the airport and anxiously awaited the security chief's arrival at the restaurant. Soon they were approached by a tall, stocky man, with distinguished features and slightly grizzled hair. Accompanying him was a thin, gray-haired man in a dark suit.

"You're the Hardy boys, I take it," said the stocky one. "I'm Dell. This is Mr. Smith."

Both men shook hands and Dell added, "Your father has told me a lot about you two. He's very proud—says his sons are great detectives."

The four entered the restaurant and seated themselves at a table by a front window. Mr. Smith kept looking down at his hands.

"Who is he?" Frank wondered.

Both boys noticed that Mr. Smith was twisting a crested gold ring on his finger.

"Looks like a school emblem," Frank thought, then suddenly realized what the man was telling him. *"He's from SKOOL!"*

Joe got the message at the same time and threw a quick glance at his brother.

Dell smiled. "I felt sure you would understand. It is safer if some things are not said aloud. Mr. Smith and I work together." So Dell was also a member of SKOOL, working under the guise of security officer for Great Circle Airways!

He went on to say that Mr. Hardy had come to him some weeks before and asked for dossiers on all employees and the passenger lists for the past two years. "I supplied the information."

Dell was interrupted for a minute while a waitress took their orders. Smith gave none. Then the security chief leaned closer.

"Your father found out that Hexton owns a castle in the north of Scotland. It's a retreat, the magician claims, where he rests and devises new tricks for his show. He goes there several times a month on our planes."

"Sounds like a great setup for smuggling secrets out of this country," Frank said softly.

"That's just what your father concluded," Smith said. "But he disappeared before he had a chance to give me a detailed report. So far nothing has been proved."

In turn, Frank and Joe quickly told about the information they had gleaned from Mr. Hardy's file on Hexton.

"Where is Dad" Frank asked urgently. "Have you any idea??"

"I had a reliable tip that Hexton has taken him to South Africa," Smith replied. "My organization will move in on the situation there." He glanced at his watch and abruptly stood up. "If you need me, contact Mr. Dell. Good luck." He walked off quietly.

A few moments later the food came. As they were eating, Joe suddenly exclaimed, "Look!" He clutched his brother's arm and pointed toward the large front window of the restaurant.

"What is it?"

"A man just peered in here! I'm sure he's Stony Bleeker!"

The boys darted outside, followed by Dell. But Bleeker was not among the passers-by.

"Maybe he ran around back!" Joe suggested.

"Quick!" Frank ordered. "Let's split up and check the building on all sides! Joe, you stay here in front! Mr. Dell, I'll take the east side, if you'll take the west!"

"Let's go!" the security chief agreed.

Frank raced along the east side of the building. Carefully he rounded the corner, but did not spot Bleeker. Just then he heard sounds of a scuffle coming from around the far side.

"*Uhff!*" someone groaned.

Frank ran to the spot to find Dell lying on the ground. He bent over the prostrate man.

"Are you all right?" Frank asked worriedly. He helped the security chief to his feet.

"I almost had him," Dell said, breathing heavily. "But he got in a fast punch." Dell pointed. "There he goes now!"

Frank turned and saw Bleeker dashing into the airport parking lot. The boy bolted after him. The man had too big a lead, though. Before Frank could reach him, Bleeker scrambled into a car and sped away. Disappointed, Frank returned to the restaurant. Dell was already there.

"Any luck?" Joe asked his brother.

"No. Didn't even get the license plate number."

"Bleeker's thin," Dell commented as he rubbed his chin, "but he packs a lot of power."

"What'll we do now?" Joe asked.

Frank thought for a moment. "We'll check the list of cities scheduled on Hexton's tour. If we can trail him without his knowing it, we might trap him into revealing where he took Dad."

"I still have a copy of the playbill from his last show," Joe recalled. "I believe his tour schedule is listed in it."

"Good thinking," Dell remarked. He instructed the boys to call him if they wanted help. Then he boarded a plane to return to the Great Circle Airways base at Westboro near New York City.

"Let's go home and check that playbill right away," Frank said.

"Hexton knows that we're on to him and his gang," Joe remarked. "Do you think he'll continue with his tour?"

"Probably not," Frank answered. "But right now it's our only chance to find him."

When they returned to their car, the Hardys were surprised to see a pencil-printed note attached to the steering wheel. Frank removed it and read the contents aloud:

" 'Mind your own business! Or you'll never see your father again!' "

CHAPTER IV

Cryptic Message

"BLEEKER must have left the warning here!" Joe exclaimed.

"That's for sure," Frank agreed. "And it's no idle threat. Besides, I have a hunch Dad wasn't taken to South Africa. Otherwise, Hexton wouldn't be so determined to keep us off the trail."

The Hardys were more eager than ever to get their investigation under way. Upon arriving home, they examined the playbill which listed the cities on the magician's tour.

"According to this list," Frank observed, "Hexton is scheduled to appear at the Tivoli Theater in Darville tomorrow."

Joe paged through the atlas and pinpointed the location of the city. "Here's Darville. It's about four hundred miles from here."

The boys telephoned Jack Wayne, pilot of Mr.

Hardy's twin-engine plane, and arranged to fly to Darville the following day. Frank and Joe had private pilot licenses, but thought it wise to have Jack along. "He's a tough man in a fight," Joe said.

When they invited Chet, he eagerly accepted. "I'll meet you at the field."

The next morning Mrs. Hardy and Aunt Gertrude nervously prepared breakfast for the young detectives.

"Now don't do anything foolish," their mother cautioned. "This Hexton fellow sounds terribly dangerous to me."

"I fear the worst!" Aunt Gertrude said, shaking her head. "Detective work involves taking too many chances. No good will come of this. I can feel it in my bones."

"Don't worry about us," Joe assured them. "Hexton might be a clever magician, but we have a few tricks of our own."

After receiving more admonitions at the doorway, the boys drove to the airport. Jack Wayne, the tanned, lean-faced pilot, was waiting for them at the plane. Chet came puffing up a few moments later. Soon they were airborne and streaking toward Darville. Two hours later they circled it and set down.

Frank rented a car and they drove directly to the theater where Hexton was scheduled to appear. As they approached the Tivoli, the boys were amazed to see a man standing on a tall ladder against the marquee, removing the big black letters which spelled out the magician's name.

Frank pulled up in front of the theater, and Joe called out, "What's going on? Hexton's first show is scheduled for tonight!"

The man on the ladder shrugged. "I only follow orders. Sorry."

He pointed to the box-office window. A cancellation notice was spread across a large poster advertising the show.

"Let's have a talk with the theater manager," Frank suggested. He parked and they hastened to a door marked "Manager L. Sardella." Joe rapped loudly.

"Come in!"

When the four entered, a small, thin man with a waxed mustache removed his feet from a desk and glowered. "Yes?"

"Mr. Sardella, where is Hexton?" Joe asked tensely.

The man arose and eyed them sharply. "You want refunds?"

"No. We're private detectives," Chet said importantly. "Where is he?"

"Hexton? That's what I'd like to know. The skunk! I'll spend the rest of the day giving refunds on my advance ticket sale, and still have no show tonight."

"Why didn't he come?" Frank asked.

"Search me. He phoned long-distance. Gave no reasons. I'll sue him!"

Sardella said that the magician had mentioned he was canceling the remainder of his tour with the exception of one last performance.

"Where?" Frank asked.

"Some little place called Granton. Don't ask me what state, because I don't know. Said they pushed up the date to tonight to accommodate him. Accommodation—bah!"

The Hardys and their friends thanked the manager and hurried back to the car. They returned to the airport and hastened to the operations room to consult a large aeronautical chart mounted on the wall.

"Here's Granton," the pilot said, pointing. He quickly plotted a course. "It's a little bit more than a thousand miles from here."

"Good grief!" Chet exclaimed. "We'll never get there in time."

Frank glanced at his watch. "We ought to be able to make the trip in under seven hours, wouldn't you say, Jack?"

The pilot manipulated a small flight computer, which he had taken from a jacket pocket. "With the present winds, I'd say we could do it in seven hours easily."

"If we take off right now," Frank said, "we can be in Granton before Hexton's show ends."

"I'm game, fellows," Chet piped up, "if you'll

let me get some chow for the trip." He trotted toward the airport cafeteria and returned a few minutes later with a bag of sandwiches and milk.

Soon the four companions were in the air, speeding toward Granton. They set down late that evening at an airport thirty miles from the town, rented a car, and started off. Fortunately, the speed limit was generous. Also, Granton had only one theater, which Frank found easily.

It was nearly time for the show to end. Frank parked the car across the street from the lighted marquee.

Joe walked down an alley to the rear and reported that there was only one other exit besides the front. "It's on the side."

"Keep a sharp lookout for Hexton and his men after the performance," Frank instructed the others. "Also, remember that they mustn't spot *us* or our chance to follow them might fail."

Twenty minutes later the show ended and people spilled out through the doors. Presently a green sedan drove up in front of the theater.

"Look!" Joe said in a loud whisper. "The driver is Stony Bleeker!"

Four men appeared from the alley exit. "There's Hexton!" Chet whispered.

"And Vordo with two short men!" Frank observed.

"They look like twins!" Joe exclaimed.

"I'll bet that's how Hexton works the vanishing bit," said Chet. "One twin disappears in the box and the other appears from the wings! From the audience, who could tell they weren't the same man?"

The magician and his assistants got into the car and sped off. Frank and his companions followed at a safe distance. Several blocks farther on, the green car passed a high wall surrounding a garden back of a hotel, then pulled around the corner and stopped in front of the Granton Inn. The men got out and entered, while a doorman drove the car into the hotel's underground garage.

Frank parked a short distance from the entrance. "Let's stay out here and see what happens," he said. "We'll take turns keeping watch. Good thing there are no exits except to this street or the garden." The foursome settled down for a long vigil.

As they waited, Joe noticed that Chet seemed preoccupied. His stout friend was staring at something high on the side of the hotel.

"What are you looking at?" Joe asked.

"That window up there near the top. The room light is going on and off."

The young sleuths watched the light for a time before noticing that it was following a definite pattern.

"Dit-dit-dit dah-dah-dah dit-dit-dit," mumbled Frank in tempo with the light.

"An SOS!" Joe cried. "In Morse code!"

"No doubt about it!" Frank exclaimed. "Maybe it's from Dad! He could be a prisoner in Hexton's room!"

Throwing caution to the winds, the Hardys dashed into the hotel. Chet and Jack Wayne remained in the car to watch the exit. The desk clerk was startled when the boys rushed in.

"Which is the Incredible Hexton's room?" Frank asked.

The man automatically answered, "He's in Suite 924. What are your names? I'll announce you."

"Never mind," Joe said.

"But I have to announce all visitors," the clerk insisted. "It's a hotel rule."

As he scooped up the house phone, Frank and Joe darted into an elevator. They burned with impatience while the car rose slowly. When it reached the ninth floor, the boys hopped out and rushed to Hexton's suite. To their surprise, the door was partly open. On it hung a sign: DO NOT DISTURB.

"Careful!" Frank warned. "It might be a trap."

Cautiously they entered and hurriedly glanced into each of the rooms of the suite.

"Nobody here!" Joe declared.

"They were warned by the desk clerk's call," Frank said. "Let's go after them! They must have escaped by a stairway."

The boys ran along the corridor toward an exit sign and bounded down the staircase. Reaching the lobby, they asked the clerk if he had seen Hexton or his assistants pass through.

"I've seen no one," was the response. "What's this all about?"

"No time to tell you now," Frank said. "How do we get to the underground garage?"

"By the elevator or the back stairs," the clerk answered.

"Quick! Outside!" Frank shouted to Joe. "Maybe we can cut them off!"

They raced from the hotel and headed for the driveway leading to the underground garage. Just then the green sedan roared out.

"Watch it!" Joe yelled. They fell backward as the speeding car grazed their jackets. Scrambling to their feet, the boys ran for their own car. It was gone!

"Chet and Jack must have recognized Hexton," Frank surmised, "and followed him."

He and Joe hurried back to the hotel to search the magician's rooms for clues.

"Come here!" Frank called softly to Joe as he opened the door to an adjoining bedroom. "This is where the SOS was sent from!" The electrical plug to a lamp was only part way in the wall outlet.

"The signal must have been sent by manipulating the plug," Frank said.

"What's that?" Joe exclaimed, pointing to something written near the base of the wall. The pair bent down to examine the faint scribbling. It read:

441810682300 *Am all right—*

"That's Dad's writing!" Joe exclaimed. "He was trying to tell us something!"

"The 'Am all right' is clear enough," Frank remarked as he carefully studied the writing. "But the numerals—what do you make of them?"

Joe rubbed his chin thoughtfully. "Nothing— yet. But I'll bet they're mighty important."

Frank took a notebook from his pocket and jotted down the cryptic message. The boys then went downstairs and walked out of the hotel just as Chet and Jack Wayne drove up.

"We chased 'em!" Chet said.

"Any luck?" Frank asked.

"No! Only their license number. Lost 'em in traffic," Jack answered.

"But," Chet continued eagerly, "we did get close enough to see that there were six men in the car."

Frank nodded. "I'm sure the sixth was Dad!"

After phoning a description and the license number of the green car to the police, Jack and the boys decided to return to the theater.

"Hexton must have left his stage equipment behind," Frank said. "Perhaps he gave instructions where he wanted it sent."

At the theater a local truck was parked near the side entrance.

"Maybe it's waiting to pick up the gear," Joe said.

"Let's ask some questions," Frank suggested.

Chet and Jack Wayne were instructed to keep an eye on the truck while the Hardys went inside. They confronted the theater manager just as he was locking his office, and asked him where Hexton's equipment was to be taken.

"As far as I know," the man replied, "Hexton made arrangements to have it stored in a local warehouse."

"Did he leave anyone behind to dismantle and pack the stuff?" Frank inquired.

"Yes—a man I never saw before. Said he had just arrived in town this morning," the manager replied. "Hexton took his four regular assistants with him."

A shout came from the street and the boys rushed outside.

Chet's face was flushed with excitement. "A man forced Jack into the truck and drove off! He had a gun!" Chet pointed down the street. "There they go!"

Frank and Joe caught a glimpse of the vehicle as it rounded a corner several blocks away. They grabbed Chet's arms and dashed for their car!

CHAPTER V

Mysterious Rendezvous

FRANK jumped behind the wheel, the doors were slammed shut, and the car roared off in pursuit of Jack Wayne's kidnapper! Seconds later, the headlights picked the truck out of the darkness on a road leading from the city.

"The driver must know we're after him," Frank observed as the vehicle speeded up. "I'll try to head him off." He bore down on the accelerator until the needle touched the speed limit.

"We're gaining!" Chet yelled. Gradually the car moved alongside the truck. Then, with a burst of power, it pulled ahead and in front.

"Be careful!" Joe pleaded. "That truck could plow right through us!"

The two vehicles reeled back and forth across the road as Frank tried frantically to prevent the truck from pulling ahead of them.

"If someone comes toward us from the opposite

direction, we've had it," Chet mumbled as he wiped his forehead.

He relaxed a bit when the speedometer indicated less than forty miles per hour. Frank had noticed that the truck had suddenly slowed and begun to wobble violently.

"What's happening?" Joe asked.

"Leaping mackerel!" Chet yelled. "Jack and the driver are fighting! Oh, I hope that man doesn't shoot!"

He had hardly finished speaking when the truck skidded off the road. *Crash!* With a thud the heavy vehicle tumbled on its side into a shallow ditch, its wheels spinning.

Frank squealed to a stop. The boys leaped out and ran to the wreck, just as Jack Wayne pushed his door open.

"Jack! You all right?" Frank panted.

"A little shaky, but this guy's been kayoed."

Jack climbed out and the others dragged the driver through the door. He regained consciousness a few moments later and weakly shook his head.

"Who are you?" Frank demanded.

"None of your business," the man muttered. He was tall and husky, with bulging muscles. He looked for his revolver, which now lay on the road.

"The police will be interested to know you kidnapped Jack Wayne," Joe said, pointing to the pilot.

"All right!" the driver bellowed. "My name is Burly Wilkes!"

"How long have you been working for Hexton?" Frank asked.

"Just today. And I didn't try to kidnap anybody!"

"I suppose you just felt like taking our friend for a ride at pistol point," Chet remarked scornfully.

"Hexton hired me to take care of his equipment," Wilkes said. "He told me there were some guys trying to steal his stuff. When I saw your friend snooping around the truck, I thought he was one of 'em. I just wanted to give him a scare."

At that moment a police car arrived on the scene. An officer jumped out and walked toward them. "What's going on here?"

When the boys explained, the officer took Wilkes into custody and requested that Jack Wayne follow him to police headquarters to file a complaint.

Further questioning of Wilkes by the police revealed nothing more than what he had already told the young detectives. Apparently, Frank reasoned, he was more afraid of Hexton than of being thrown into jail.

The Hardys and their companions checked in at a motel to get a little sleep. Early the next morning they flew back to Bayport. Chet said good-by and headed for the farm in his jalopy.

Mrs. Hardy and Aunt Gertrude were overjoyed to see Frank and Joe, and instantly asked about Mr. Hardy. They received a detailed report.

"I'm still fearful," said the boys' mother, "but the news is somewhat encouraging. You say he wrote, 'Am all right—'?"

"Yes," Frank assured her.

Aunt Gertrude said in her forceful way, "That's enough for me. I'm sure Fenton is a better magician than Hexton when it comes to escaping from traps. He'll get out of those villains' clutches!"

"You're right," Joe agreed. "Just the same, I think he needs our help."

Directly after supper Frank and Joe went to their father's study and tried to decipher the message scribbled on the hotel wall.

Joe read aloud, " '441810682300.' "

"I'm stymied," Frank admitted. "The numbers don't fit into any code Dad's used with us before."

"Maybe it isn't a code at all," Joe suggested. "The numbers might represent something else."

Just then Chet arrived. He strolled into the study with a large silver bowl tucked under one arm. In his other hand he held a big square of blue silk.

"Okay, you masterminds! Give me your attention!" he demanded. "You see standing before you the dean of sorcerers! The master of legerdemain! The world's most outstanding thauma—thauma—thaumaturgist!"

"Wow!" Joe exclaimed. "Listen to him! You'd better get the dictionary, Frank!"

Chet placed the bowl on the desk as the Hardys watched in amusement. "You are most fortunate," he said, "since you will see a private performance by the great—the incredible—the fantastic Morton!"

Chet paused, a faint smile curling his lips and added, "Perhaps you hadn't heard that I've been taking a mail-order course in magic!"

The Hardys looked unimpressed and said nothing. Chet eyed them with a smug expression. "Will you please bring me an egg, some relish, mustard, catsup, and perhaps some vinegar and water."

"Yes, master!" Joe left the study and returned shortly with the items. "Here you are." He grinned. "And whatever you plan to do with them it had better be good. Aunt Gertrude almost took the broom to me for bringing this stuff."

Ignoring Joe's remark, the chubby youth con-

tinued with his spiel. "All right! Prepare yourselves for the impossible!" he declared. "Listen
now to my weird and strange incantations!
Utterances that will mystify the ages!"

The boys watched as Chet cracked the egg and
dropped it into the bowl, shell and all. He added
the vinegar, water, and other ingredients.

"What a crazy concoction!" Joe said as his
chum stirred the mixture.

Chet covered the bowl with the silk cloth.
"Brace yourselves for the most amazing feat of all
time!" He began to pass his hands slowly over the
bowl. *"Ezard, Kazard Mokim, Whumpf!"*

"Now what" Frank asked.

"Ah!" Chet announced. "You have just wit-
nessed an astounding display of my mystical
powers! The ingredients in this bowl have vanished. *Puhff!* Just like that!"

"Okay, Merlin," Joe said, laughing. "Prove it.
Uncover the bowl."

"You doubt my magical skills?" Chet said. "I
won't just uncover the bowl—I'll go a step further
to prove my powers." He placed the bowl on his
head upside down.

"There! You see, I—" He stopped short as its
contents flowed over his head and face. Some
spattered on the floor. "Oh, ugh!"

The Hardys howled with laughter. "You'd better clean up that mess fast," Frank warned. "If

Frank and Joe howled with laughter

Aunt Gertrude sees it she'll cause *you* to vanish. *Puhff!* Just like that!"

Joe rushed out of the study and returned with an armful of paper towels. It took considerable rubbing before Chet became recognizable again and the carpet clean.

"I can't understand," he murmured. "The book said it would work!"

Joe chuckled. "Maybe you got your incantations mixed."

"Anyway, I was just trying to cheer you fellows up," Chet mumbled.

"We appreciate that," Frank said. "But how about less spectacular tricks for a while?"

At a loss for words, Chet sat down in an armchair and examined his silver bowl.

The ringing of the telephone broke the silence in the study. Frank took the call. "Frank Hardy speaking."

"If you and your brother want to see your father," said a muffled voice, "come to the old Landon Mansion in an hour. And come alone!"

"Who is this?" Frank demanded. There was a sharp clicking sound. The mysterious caller had hung up!

The message startled the boys. "Did you recognize the voice?" Joe asked.

"I'm not sure," Frank said, "but it sounded like Hexton's giant helper, Vordo!"

"The Landon Mansion, eh?" Joe queried.

"That old dilapidated house hasn't been lived in for years. I understand it'll be torn down soon."

"If I remember correctly, it's just off Highway 18," Frank recalled. "It'll take us about thirty minutes to drive there."

"But it may be a trap!" Joe declared.

"We must take the risk," Frank insisted. "Dad really might be there."

They asked Chet to post himself at the telephone. "If we're not back in two hours, notify the police," Frank requested.

He and Joe stopped to tell Mrs. Hardy their plans. Though worried, she conceded they should go. Ten minutes later the Hardys' car was humming down the highway on the outskirts of town. The night was clear and a strong breeze lent a chill to the air. A full moon bathed the trees and fields in an eerie, silvery light.

Before long, the Hardys came to a narrow dirt road and turned onto it. Neglected for many years, it was pitted with holes and covered in spots with clumps of grass and weeds. There were signs, however, that some kind of vehicle had traveled the road recently. Much of the grass had been flattened and there were tire tracks.

At the end of the rutted road, the two sleuths discovered iron gateposts. The gates had long since fallen from their rusted hinges. In the distance stood the Landon Mansion, ghostly in the moonlight. Frank and Joe got out of the car and walked toward it. The only light came from a window on the second floor.

Reaching the house, they stopped and listened for a moment. All was quiet.

The Hardys furtively made their way to the door and eased it open. Silently they slipped in, but froze like statues when Vordo's voice boomed from upstairs.

"Your father's waiting here!"

Frank and Joe broke into a cold sweat. "That guy must have radar eyes," Frank whispered. "Come on, Joe! We can't turn back now."

The boys climbed the creaky staircase, which groaned under their feet. Just before they reached the top, a grinding sound echoed through the old building. With a splintering crash the staircase parted just where they were standing. The lower section fell away and the boys plunged toward the darkness below!

CHAPTER VI

Aerial Chase

FALLING, Frank made a grab for the step ahead of him and hung on as Joe gripped his waist. Though his arms ached from the strain, Frank pulled desperately, hoisting himself up inch by inch.

Finally Joe reached out and grasped the step. After much effort, both boys worked themselves safely onto the next tread.

"These guys don't play around," Frank murmured, rubbing his swollen hands. "Well, up we go."

They climbed the few remaining steps and entered the room straight ahead. It was empty, except for a small table, on which a single candle burned.

At the end of the room was a window. The boys rushed to it and looked down into the yard in time to see Vordo and Stony Bleeker leap into a car and speed off.

"Neat getaway," Joe muttered.

"No use trying to chase them," Frank said. "They'll be out of sight by the time we get to our car."

"Dad wasn't with them," Joe commented.

"Of course not. Calling us over here *was* just a trap," Frank replied. He pulled angrily on the rope which Vordo and Bleeker had used to get from the window to the ground.

The boys went to examine the remaining section of the staircase. It had been sawed more than halfway through! In a sober mood Frank and Joe returned to the window, slid down the rope, then drove home. Chet was greatly relieved to see his friends.

"What about your dad?" he asked excitedly, and was quickly told what had happened.

"Wow! Well, I'm glad you're safe," Chet said. "While you were gone two important phone calls came in. The first was from the police chief in Granton. He said Burly Wilkes has escaped!"

"What!" Joe exclaimed. "How did that happen?"

"A detective had handcuffed Wilkes to a table in the interrogation room while he went out for a few minutes," Chet said. "When he returned, Wilkes was gone. Somehow, he had slipped out of the handcuffs."

"A trick he could have learned from Hexton," Frank mused.

"And another thing," Chet went on, "the green sedan was Hexton's and it has not been picked up."

"What about the second call?"

"It was from Kenneth Dell," Chet answered. "He wants to talk to you as soon as possible."

Frank picked up the phone and dialed the private number of the Great Circle Airways' security chief.

Dell sounded excited. "I've had a report that one of our flight stewards, named Timken, has been acting suspicious lately. He used to be friendly and stay around for a while after landing. Now shortly after he gets in from Scotland on Flight 101, he leaves in a waiting helioplane. He never says where he's going."

"That is strange," Frank remarked. "A helioplane! The kind that can take off and land in short distances?"

"Right! It can also fly at very low speeds."

"Have you any idea where the steward goes?" Frank asked.

"No flight plan was filed," Dell said.

"Who owns the plane?" Joe inquired.

"I don't know, but now I mean to find out," Dell replied. "Whenever the pilot has asked for landing instructions, he has identified himself as 'Helioplane 345.' Of course those are only the last three figures in his whole number."

Joe asked, "What about Timken as a steward?"

"He was hired by our firm only a couple of months ago. Seems efficient and so far we haven't found anything incriminating in his record. Flight 101 is part of his regular schedule, and I'm watching it for anything the least bit suspicious. With Hexton's headquarters probably in a Scottish castle, we can't be too careful about our Scotland flights."

"I have an idea," said Frank. "The next time Timken takes the helioplane, Joe and I will follow him."

"Follow him?" Dell said. "How?"

"In Dad's plane."

"But if you were to take off immediately behind the helioplane and trail it on the same course," Dell countered, "wouldn't that arouse the pilot's suspicions?"

"We would take off from a different airport," Frank said. "Hold on just a minute, will you?"

He beckoned Joe, who handed him an aeronautical chart. Spreading it out, Frank examined the area in the vicinity of Great Circle's base. Then he picked up the phone again.

"There's a small general airfield at Burnsbie near your base," he told Dell. "We'll land there and wait. When you see the steward boarding the helioplane, let us know."

"It might just work at that," the SKOOL agent agreed.

"What is Timken's first name and when is he

scheduled to return from his next flight?" Frank asked.

"Stand by. I'll check the crew schedule." There was a brief pause, then Dell came on again. "His first name is Guy, and he's scheduled for an outgoing flight tonight. He'll be back here at ten o'clock Thursday morning, our time."

"Good!" Frank said. "Barring bad weather, we'll plan to be at the field at least an hour before Timken is due back."

Frank said good-by, then called Jack Wayne and informed him of the plan. The pilot said he would have the plane fueled and ready to fly Thursday morning at the crack of dawn.

As the first rays of sunlight appeared in the east that day, the Hardys got up and dressed. They were surprised to find their mother and Aunt Gertrude already in the kitchen preparing breakfast for them.

"Um! Sausage and cakes!" Joe said with a grin.

Immediately after breakfast, the boys drove to Bayport Airport. There they made a final check on the weather. The forecaster told them it would be CAVU—Ceiling and Visibility Unlimited—for at least another forty-eight hours.

"The ship's all set to fly!" Jack Wayne called as they walked across the ramp.

He and the Hardys got into the plane and fastened their seat belts. A sudden roar echoed across the field as Jack started engines. He made a quick but thorough check of the instruments. Minutes later, they were airborne and climbing rapidly above Bayport.

"We should get to Burnsbie with plenty of time to spare," Frank said as he glanced at his watch.

Upon arriving at their destination, Jack attended to the refueling of the plane, while Frank and Joe waited in the operations room for a call from Kenneth Dell.

It was a few minutes after ten o'clock when the telephone rang. The airport manager scooped up the receiver, then announced that the call was for the boys.

"This is Kenneth Dell, Frank! Timken just got into the helioplane. They're taxiing out now for take-off."

"Roger!" declared the young detective. "We're on our way."

In a matter of minutes, Jack Wayne and the Hardys were approaching Great Circle's base at several thousand feet.

"There's the helioplane!" Joe exclaimed. "It's at the three-o'clock position."

The craft veered slightly to a northeast course. Jack followed at a safe distance.

A short time later the helioplane made two complete turns, then reverted to course. Jack did the same. Moments later, their quarry repeated the maneuver.

"Why all those turns?" Joe asked.

"He's probably checking to see if he's being followed," Jack replied.

"Do you suppose he spotted us?" Joe asked.

Frank replied, "No doubt. But we've nothing to lose by continuing the chase."

The gap between the two crafts, however, decreased more and more as the helioplane reduced speed.

"That clunker up ahead can fly much slower than we can." Jack's voice showed concern.

He attempted to keep his distance, but another glance at the airspeed indicator told him that their plane was dangerously near to a stall. The Hardys tightened their seat belts when the craft began to buffet.

"Sorry, boys," the pilot said. "I can't make it." He was about to increase power when suddenly the helioplane executed a sharp turn and headed directly for them. Jack quickly maneuvered out of the way, but the sharp movement of the controls caused the aircraft to stall.

The plane rolled into an almost inverted position and dived vertically toward the ground!

CHAPTER VII

Suspect on the Run

FRANK and Joe were thrown against their seat belts as the plane dropped earthward, and the wind whistled an eerie dirge against the wings.

"Hang on!" Jack shouted as he pulled the throttle closed and applied aileron and rudder control.

He managed to level the wings, then concentrated on recovering from the steep dive. As he eased back slowly on the wheel, the boys were pressed down into their seats by the increasing G force.

Finally Jack had the aircraft back to straight and level—but with not much altitude to spare. He increased power and the plane climbed higher. For a moment nobody spoke.

"Whew!" Joe finally exclaimed as he wiped perspiration from his face. "I can't say I'm too keen on this kind of maneuver."

"Whoever is flying that helioplane," Jack Wayne remarked, "is a pretty good pilot."

"Keep a sharp lookout," Frank urged as he searched the sky above them.

They continued to gain altitude and the boys scanned the area on all sides. Ahead, puffy white cumulus clouds built up over the hilly terrain.

"I'm afraid we've lost our quarry," the pilot said. "And I'll bet they're members of UGLI!"

"Yes, worse luck," Frank answered. "The clouds offer excellent cover. Trying to find those agents in it would be like trying to find a flea in a fog."

The Hardys decided to discontinue the chase and return to Great Circle's base. Upon landing, an announcement came over the public-address system.

"Frank and Joe Hardy, please report to the operations room."

The young sleuths sprinted to the administration building. In the operations room Kenneth Dell was clutching a telephone to his ear.

"What's up?" Frank asked.

"Flight Service has just given me the helioplane's full registration number. I told them to let me know if they heard anything from the pilot," Dell said. "Looks as if we're in luck! He ran into bad weather north of here, and had to file an instrument flight plan."

"What's his destination?" Joe asked.

"Logan International Airport, Boston," the security chief replied.

"Jeepers!" Joe exclaimed. "Do you think that's where he was headed all the time?"

"I doubt it," Frank replied. "Timken wouldn't want anyone to know where he's going. I think they're just planning to land and wait for the weather to clear. Then they can continue the trip without a flight plan."

Dell signaled for silence as he pressed the receiver closer to his ear. He jotted down a few notes and then hung up.

"Here's something else," he announced. "The pilot's name given on the flight plan is Mazer. And the owner of the helioplane is the Coastal Courier Service."

"Say," Joe spoke up, "why don't we have Jack fly us to Boston right away? Logan is a busy airport. Timken might not notice our arrival."

"Good idea," Dell said. "In the meantime, I'm going to check out this information."

An hour and a half later Jack Wayne and the boys were cleared for an ILS approach at Logan International Airport.

"Looks as if the weather's beginning to improve," Jack remarked as they taxied to the parking ramp.

"I don't see the helioplane anywhere," Joe observed.

"We'll check with operations," Frank said.

The boys hurried into the administration building. They located the operations manager and inquired about the helioplane.

"Why, yes," he said. "I remember the craft distinctly. It caught my eye, since that kind of thing is a rarity around here."

"Where is it now?" Joe asked.

"I think it took off about thirty minutes ago," the operations manager replied. "But why don't you check with the control tower?" He pointed to a wall telephone. "That's a direct line."

Frank picked up the phone.

"Logan Tower! Stigand speaking!" crackled from the receiver.

Frank said, "A helioplane departed from here about half an hour ago. Can you tell me its destination?"

"Stand by!"

There were a few seconds of silence, then Stigand reported, "The pilot filed an instrument flight plan for Concord Airport, New Hampshire. However, he broke into clear weather at Manchester and canceled his flight plan."

"Thank you," Frank replied, dejected.

"So we've lost them again," Joe remarked.

"Timken and his pilot played it smart," Frank said. "They knew they'd fly into clear weather. I'll bet they never had any intention of landing at Concord."

Just then two men approached the youths.

"What's your interest in the helioplane?" one of them demanded.

"Who are you?" Joe retorted.

"We're detectives! Boston Police Department!" They flashed their badges.

"My name is Amory," one said. He pointed to his partner. "And this is Detective Sergeant Doran."

Frank introduced himself and his companions.

"Hardy!" Amory exclaimed. "Any relation to Fenton Hardy the private detective?"

"We're his sons," Joe answered.

"Why did you ask us about our interest in the helioplane?" Frank inquired.

"A couple of hours ago a local jeweler was approached by a fellow who tried to sell him a diamond. When the jeweler began to question him as to where he got it, the guy walked out. The jeweler became suspicious and called us."

"What started you looking for this man at the airport?" Joe asked.

Amory replied, "The jeweler said he was wearing a Great Circle Airways uniform. So the airport seemed a logical place to begin a search, although Great Circle doesn't come in here. We want to ask that fellow a few questions."

"He's gone," Frank said. "The man you're looking for is the same one we've been following. He took off in the helioplane about half an hour ago."

"That adds up," Doran commented. "The operations manager told us a fellow answering the jeweler's description had already left."

"We approached you boys," Ames added, "because we heard you inquiring on the phone about the helioplane."

There was little more the young sleuths could do, so they took off. During the return flight to Bayport, they mulled over the latest event.

"What do you make of Timken trying to peddle a diamond?" Joe asked.

"It sounds to me like an attempt to get rid of stolen goods," Frank concluded.

"Could be," Joe said thoughtfully. "You remember Dad's report said that Hexton's gang were robbers. If Timken is one of them, he may be smuggling in jewels stolen overseas and disposing of them here."

Frank agreed. "But UGLI's business is espionage. I doubt if they would become involved in jewel robberies. On the other hand, Hexton and his gang might be playing the two games at once."

When the boys arrived home, Frank at once telephoned their suspicions to Kenneth Dell.

"You have a good theory there," Great Circle's security chief said. "I'm going to call Scotland Yard and inquire about recent jewel robberies." He promised to get in touch later.

After Frank hung up the phone, he stood silent for a moment. "Next we *must* figure out that message Dad left on the hotel wall," he told Joe.

Again they examined the row of numerals: 441810682300. But after more than an hour of attempting to decipher them, Joe gave a sigh of frustration. "It doesn't make any more sense to me now than when we first started," he admitted.

"If this is a code, it's a real puzzler," Frank agreed. "But we've *got* to crack it!"

When Mrs. Hardy announced that dinner was ready, the boys reluctantly interrupted their task. They ate quickly, then went right back to the message.

Frank stared at it. "Neither the substitution nor transposition ciphers jibe."

The young detectives worked late into the night. Exhausted, they finally went to bed.

Early the next day Frank and Joe continued to study the message, but all their efforts to decipher it ended in failure.

Shortly after ten o'clock Chet arrived at the Hardys' home. He plodded up the stairs to the detective's study.

"You're too late for breakfast, chum," Frank said with a grin.

"Aw, cut it out," Chet mumbled. "Anyway, I stopped at Biff Hooper's house before I came here. His mother was baking the most delicious pancakes I ever saw, with sausages and all the trimmings."

"Glad to hear that," Joe said jokingly. "We wouldn't want to see you fade away."

"How is Biff?" Frank inquired as he glanced at his friend. Biff Hooper was a schoolmate of the boys at Bayport High.

"He's just fine. I wanted to show him a couple of my magic tricks."

"Don't tell us you took that silver bowl of yours along?" Joe asked.

"No, that's old stuff," Chet retorted. "My new tricks are more sophisticated."

"Oh yeah!" said Joe, chuckling.

"Go ahead and laugh if you want to," Chet continued indignantly. "At least Biff appreciated the great latitude of my genius."

At Chet's remark, Frank sat bolt upright in his chair.

"What's the matter?" Chet asked, startled.

"Would you repeat what you just said?" Frank asked excitedly.

"You mean about Biff's appreciating the latitude of my genius?"

Frank sprang up. "The key! You've given me the key!"

CHAPTER VIII

Sailing Sleuths

CHET looked confused. "What key? I don't see any key," he said, glancing around.

"You mentioned latitude! That must be it—latitude and longitude!" Frank pointed to the numerals in the mystery message.

"I still don't get it," said Chet.

Frank explained. "Notice that there are a total of twelve digits. The first six—441810—must mean 44 degrees, 18 minutes, 10 seconds of latitude. The remaining figures—682300—would then stand for 68 degrees, 23 minutes, 00 seconds of longitude "

"You're right!" Joe exclaimed.

Frank riffled through a stack of maps and selected one showing the Atlantic seaboard. "Those coordinates would locate a position in the area covered by this map."

"Hold on!" Joe said as he glanced at a chart

of the world that he had just unfolded. "The message doesn't specify whether the latitude is east or west, or the longitude north or south. Therefore, these coordinates might designate a location in Asia, the southern tip of South America, or the middle of the Indian Ocean."

"True," Frank agreed. "But since Dad didn't make that clear in the message, I'm certain he means the position is in our own hemisphere."

He marked the spot on his map indicated by the coordinates. It was about eighteen miles off the northeast coast of the United States.

"But that's a spot in the Atlantic Ocean!" Joe exclaimed.

Frank pulled out a nautical chart. It was on a smaller scale and showed more detail. Replotting the position, he discovered several small islets in the vicinity—so small they did not have names. The latitude and longitude coordinates lay directly over one.

"Eureka!" Joe exclaimed. "It looks as if we're onto something! My guess is one of two possibilities—either the place is UGLI's headquarters for the U.S., or else it's where Dad was taken."

"Maybe it's both," Joe added. "We'd better make a trip to that island!"

"What about me?" Chet demanded. "Can I come, too? After all, I found the key!"

Frank bowed toward his chum. "It'll be a pleasure to have you along, genius," he said. "We might need your help." Then he walked to the telephone. "I'll call Jack and tell him to have the plane ready tomorrow morning."

When Frank told the pilot their destination, Jack assured him there were several aviation radio facilities in the vicinity that would permit them to pinpoint the islet from the air.

Early the following day the Hardys, Chet, and Jack were winging their way toward the mystery spot. Soon they paralleled the Atlantic coast.

"How long do you estimate it'll take us to reach the place?" Frank asked Jack.

The pilot checked the bearings indicated by the radio compass and omni-navigation receiver, then thumbed his small computer. "I'd say about thirty minutes from our present position."

The boys gazed below. Ocean waves broke against the craggy coastline, tracing it with a ribbon of white foam that stretched as far as the eye could see.

As they passed over a small sailboat, Joe took out binoculars and scanned the area below. "Little islands ahead," he announced, and soon the others made out small sprinkles of land dotting the surface of the water.

"According to the cross bearings I calculated," Jack announced, "we should be over the place you want within one minute."

"And what exactly are we looking for?" Chet queried.

"I don't know," Frank answered. "But if—"

"Hey!" Joe interrupted. "I see a lighthouse on that islet just below us."

Frank took the binoculars. "You're right. It appears to be abandoned, but there are several cylindrical-shaped objects just to the left of the lighthouse."

Jack took the plane to a lower altitude and Frank readjusted the glasses. "They look like drums of oil, or gasoline," he said.

"But for what?" Joe questioned. "A boat? Certainly couldn't be for an airplane."

The pilot asked for the binoculars and studied the islet. "The surface is level enough for a plane," he observed, "but it's much too short to be used as a runway—that is, except for a helicopter, or perhaps a helioplane!"

Frank and Joe glanced at each other. Could there be a connection between the islet and the helioplane in which Timken had eluded them?

Frank suggested they fly back to the coast and land at the nearest airport. "I want to find out about the islet," he said.

Jack found a small field not far inland and set the plane down. The Hardys hopped out and hastened to the operations shack. There they met a solid, middle-aged man with a shock of gray hair, who introduced himself as Ty Carter, the owner of the airport.

"I don't know much about that islet with the

abandoned lighthouse," Carter told them, "except that it is private property. It was sold at auction recently."

"Have you any idea who bought it?" Joe asked.

"Fellow named Bodkins. He's not from around here so I can't tell you anything about him."

"Bodkins?" Frank thought. A possibility struck him. "Could this be an alias of Hexton's?" Aloud he questioned, "Have you ever seen a helioplane in the vicinity of the islet?"

"Funny you should mention that," Carter replied. "During the past couple of weeks I saw one headed in that direction several times. But whether it was going to the islet or not, I wouldn't know."

The boys thanked the man for his cooperation, then returned to the plane.

"Fellows," Frank said suddenly, "I have an idea. Why don't we rent a boat and look at the place?"

"What if Hexton and his men *are* on the islet?" Chet asked.

"That's a chance we'll have to take."

After lunch Jack remained with the plane, while Chet and the Hardys hiked to the nearby coastal town. They found a boat-rental place, but unfortunately all the power craft were in use. Frank finally selected a small jib-headed racer.

He manned the helm while Joe and Chet hauled the sails to the top of the mast. A strong breeze carried them quickly away from the dock. Nearly three hours passed before the islet appeared off the port bow of their craft.

"Seems deserted," Joe said.

Frank manipulated the helm to direct the boat in a wide circle around the tiny point of land. From the other side of the islet a fast powerboat appeared.

When it drew closer, Joe exclaimed, "That's Stony Bleeker at the wheel! And Vordo's with him. They must have spotted us!"

"The boat's going to ram ours!" Chet shouted as the craft headed directly for the sailboat.

Frank applied hard helm and changed course quickly. The powerboat missed the stern by a few inches and threw a heavy spray of water over the boys. Its wake rocked the sailboat violently.

"Hold fast!" Frank cried out. "Stay in the center, fellows, or we'll capsize!"

"Look!" Joe yelled. "They've turned and they're coming at us again!"

As the powerboat sped perilously close, more water foamed over the gunwales.

"We can't stay upright much longer!" Joe shouted.

The next pass by the powerboat was so close that the two craft sideswiped. The boys hung on, but plunged into the sea an instant later as the sailboat went over on its side.

Vordo burst into wild laughter. Stony was so

preoccupied watching the boys come to the surface he failed to notice that he was steering directly toward the islet.

"Watch out!" Vordo bellowed at him.

Bleeker made a desperate, last-minute effort to turn away. Too late!

Crash!

The powerboat's momentum carried it onto the craggy shore, and a sharp rock ripped through its hull.

The men leaped out. Furious, they shook their fists. "We'll get you for this!" Vordo thundered at the three boys, who now lay across the half-overturned hull of the sailboat.

"Now what?" Chet asked.

Frank and Joe were glumly silent. They knew that trying to right their boat with its water-soaked sails would be next to impossible and the only haven within swimming distance was the islet!

CHAPTER IX

The Lighthouse Prison

In a split second Frank had made up his mind. "Quick!" he shouted. "Help me haul in the mainsail! It's our best bet."

Joe unfastened the lanyard while the other two with great effort pulled the top of the partially submerged sail down the mast. When they had it tightly lashed around the boom, the boys secured the working jib.

"Jumping catfish!" Chet yelled in alarm. "We're drifting closer to the islet!"

While he and Joe watched the movements of Vordo and Bleeker, Frank swam to the other side of the boat. He put his weight against the bottom of the keel and tried to force it downward into the water.

"Push up hard on the mast!" he shouted to Joe and Chet.

The power of their combined efforts started to rotate the sailboat.

"Harder!" Frank yelled. "Push up harder!"

Suddenly the boat rolled to an upright position. Frank reached for a hand bail-out pump clamped against the inside of the hull. Working frantically, he pumped the water out of the boat. Then he flung himself over the gunwales, followed by Joe and Chet.

"They're taking off!" Vordo bellowed to Bleeker. "After 'em!"

The two men plunged into the water and swam toward the three boys.

"Up with the sails!" Frank commanded. "I'll take the helm."

Joe and Chet hoisted the sails into place. A strong breeze caught them and began pushing the boat ahead. Frank turned the craft sharply away from the islet.

Vordo screamed at them furiously, "Stop!"

"He seems to be the excitable type," Chet said, weak with relief, as they went speeding back toward the mainland.

"We certainly didn't win that battle," Joe observed wryly. "We're retreating."

Frank nodded. "We'll have to find another way to get here, and fast," he declared. "If Dad's a prisoner in the lighthouse, they'll probably move him out as quickly as they can."

The boat had covered nearly half the distance to the mainland when the sails became almost limp.

"The wind is dying down," Joe said, alarmed. "We're barely moving."

Gradually the breeze subsided to a complete calm. The sailboat ceased to move ahead and rocked gently with the waves. Frank grabbed a paddle that was clamped under the gunwale. "Guess we'll have to get back the hard way."

"It'll take us all night at this rate!" Chet exclaimed. "There can't be much more than another hour or so of daylight."

"We have no choice," Frank said. "Let's take turns paddling."

Chet's prediction proved to be right. It was well into the night before they could see the vague outline of docks strung along the coast.

Presently they heard the put-put of an outboard motor and a bright beam of light swept the surface of water ahead. As the boat drew closer, they recognized the pilot as the man who had rented them the sailboat.

"Hey!" he shouted. "You said you wanted the boat for the day, not for the night!"

"Right." Frank grinned. "We were becalmed. How about giving us a tow to your dock?"

The man threw them a line and went on, "I've been searching for you guys since dark. In an hour I was going to notify the Coast Guard."

"I'm sorry," Frank said.

When they reached land, the boatman saw that the youths were totally exhausted. "I have extra bunks in my shack," he said. "It'll be daylight in another couple of hours. Why don't you lads eat a bite, then get some sleep?" The boys accepted his offer gratefully.

Before turning in, Frank called the airport and asked to speak to Jack.

"I was worried about you fellows," the pilot said with deep concern. "I've been waiting here in the operations shack, wondering what happened. I almost notified the police."

Frank told him of the day's adventure, then suggested that they meet in the morning for breakfast.

It was five o'clock when Frank was awakened by the sound of a motor. He climbed from his bunk and peered out the window. What he saw caused him to snap wide awake. Vordo and Bleeker in their powerboat! "They must have made temporary repairs," he thought.

Frank awakened his companions. "Wh-what's the matter?" Chet mumbled, rubbing his eyes.

"Look!" Frank said, pointing to the boat. It was just docking at a pier where a sign read: CLARK'S BOAT REPAIRS.

"That's it!" Joe declared. "They're having the hull fixed." An idea flashed through his mind. "Now would be a good time to return to the islet!"

"Don't tell me we're going to paddle ourselves all the way," Chet complained.

"We'll rent a motorboat," Frank said. He made arrangements for the craft, then telephoned the airport and explained his plan to Jack. "Vordo and Stony Bleeker just arrived with their damaged powerboat. It's docked at Clark's Boat Repair place. Could you rent a car, drive down here, and keep an eye on those two? If they should start back to the islet before we return, fly out and warn us by making a low pass. If they start to leave town, notify the authorities."

"Wilco!" the pilot replied. "I'll get going right away."

When the boys went to the dock, the owner said, "Fellows, I've just learned by radio there's some bad weather in store—a nor'easter." He pointed toward a darkening ridge of clouds far off on the horizon. "You can see it stirring up already."

"But this is important!" Frank insisted.

The boatman pondered for a moment. "Well, if you promise to keep a sharp eye to the weather and to pull into land if it starts blowing too much, I guess you can have a boat."

The boys thanked him and after a quick breakfast started out to the islet. The trip took less than half the time it had required in the sailboat. Nevertheless, when the lighthouse came into view, the sky had grown dark and the howling wind had developed into gale force.

"A hurricane!" Chet cried out.

Torrential rain burst upon the boys and the boat was tossed around like a cork in the heavy seas. But Frank skillfully kept it headed for the islet and finally maneuvered close to shore.

Joe tied the mooring line around his waist and leaped into the water. He swam hard to the craggy shore and soon had the boat on solid ground.

"Whew!" Chet groaned. "It's going to take me a month to dry out."

The boys peered through the sweeping sheets of rain at the lighthouse. Frank signaled his companions to be silent as they crept toward a lighted window near the base of the structure. Peering inside, they saw a man seated at a table.

"Burly Wilkes!" Joe whispered.

"He's alone," Frank observed. "That's a break for us."

"But what about Dad?" Joe asked.

"If they're holding him prisoner here," Frank said, "he's in another room."

"Let me take a look," Chet suggested, and stretched higher for a glimpse inside. He slipped on a rock and banged his head against the glass. Burly Wilkes whirled around.

"Hide!" Frank ordered.

As Wilkes stomped to the window, the boys flattened themselves against the wall. Apparently satisfied nothing was wrong, he returned to his chair.

"A hurricane!" Chet cried out

"That was close," Joe commented.

"Sorry," Chet mumbled sheepishly. "Now what?"

Frank whispered a plan. "We'll break in and take Wilkes by surprise. When I give the signal, hit the door with all you've got."

The boys positioned themselves. Frank raised his hand slowly, then dropped it. The three threw themselves against the door and it burst open. Wilkes jumped up from his chair, too startled to utter a cry.

"Stay where you are!" Frank commanded.

But Wilkes, recognizing the Hardys, bolted for a staircase which spiraled up to the top of the lighthouse. The boys raced after him.

Reaching the top, Wilkes rushed through a doorway and started to swing the metal door closed behind him. But Joe managed to prevent it from slamming shut by jumping into the narrow opening.

"There he goes!" Chet shouted as he spotted Wilkes running out onto a catwalk encircling the top of the structure.

Finally the fugitive could go no farther. He was trapped and turned to face his pursuers. He threw a punch but missed. Frank countered with a blow to the stomach that sent the man sprawling. In a flash, Joe and Chet were on him and Wilkes was pinned helplessly to the metal grating of the catwalk.

"Let go of me!" he screeched.

Frank motioned the other two off, then dragged the man to his feet. "Hexton kidnapped our father, didn't he?"

"Yes. But I had nothing to do with it!"

"Where are they keeping him?"

"He *was* here."

"Was?"

"Well, he's gone!"

"Where?"

"I don't know. Mr. Hardy escaped more than five days ago. Those SKOOL men are pretty smart!"

CHAPTER X

Wing Signal

THE boys were dumfounded. "What do you mean our dad escaped?" Joe asked. "How?"

"I don't know. I wasn't here."

Frank believed that Wilkes was telling the truth. But where could their father be? And why hadn't he been in touch with them?

The Hardys tied Wilkes securely to a chair. Then Frank, Joe, and Chet settled down to wait out the storm.

While the wind and rain beat against the lighthouse, Frank and Joe questioned Wilkes further. Their prisoner said he did not know the whereabouts of Hexton, nor just what sort of an operation he was running.

"I'm a new man in the outfit. The magician hasn't taken me into his confidence," he added.

"So you're just learning the UGLI business," Frank remarked. Wilkes nodded.

He admitted that the metal drums which the Hardys had spotted contained airplane fuel, but now were empty. This was confirmed by Joe's thorough search as soon as the rain subsided and the sun burst through the broken clouds.

"Okay, Wilkes," Frank said tersely when his brother returned. "You told the truth about the drums. What about the helioplane?"

The man's jaw dropped. "Wh-what'd you mean—helioplane?"

"You know all right!" Joe said. "So far, we've made things easy for you, Wilkes, but if you don't tell the whole story, we'll have you charged as an accomplice to a kidnapping!"

"No, no!" he whined, blanching a sickly white. "I saw the plane land here twice. Both times it stayed a few minutes, then took off again."

"Were there any passengers aboard?"

"Just one guy wearing some kind of uniform." The man began to perspire freely. "Hexton will kill me if he finds out I told you."

"Don't worry about him," Chet said. "The Hardys will take care of that crooked magician."

Just then they heard an airplane and rushed outside. Looking up, they saw their own plane coming in from the west. It dived and made a low pass over the islet

"The signal!" Frank exclaimed. "Vordo and Bleeker must be on their way back!"

"Let's wait and nab 'em," Joe suggested.

Frank was about to answer when Jack Wayne headed in toward the islet again. He made another low pass, but this time the boys saw a small object drop from the plane. It bounced along the rocky surface and rolled to a stop close by. It was a metal box with a message inside:

Vordo and Bleeker on way back! Have two other men with them. Believe they are armed. Suggest you leave immediately. Head north before turning toward mainland to avoid their boat.

"Let's get out of here fast!" Chet said.

"I don't like the idea of running," Frank said, "but the odds are against us. We'll go back to the mainland and notify the police."

Pushing the reluctant Wilkes before them, the boys hastened to their motorboat. Luckily it was undamaged by the storm. A quick check of the fuel, however, showed they could not take the northerly course Jack had suggested.

"We have just enough gas to make shore," Frank announced.

"What about Vordo and his men?" Chet asked.

"Maybe we'll be able to slip by without their noticing us," Frank answered.

Wilkes became arrogant at hearing that his cohorts were on their way back. "You'd better leave me behind if you know what's good for you," he growled.

"Nothing doing," Joe retorted angrily. "And don't try to attract the attention of your buddies. I'm sure they'd reward you for having talked," he added sarcastically.

This frightened Wilkes. He slumped down.

While Jack circled overhead, the boys made a beeline for the coast. A little more than half an hour had passed, when Jack throttled the engines on and off several times.

"Is he having trouble?" Chet asked.

The pilot gunned the engines again.

"No!" Joe exclaimed. "He's signaling us!" Joe pointed to a small object in the distance, moving across the water. "That must be Vordo!"

Frank quickly turned the motorboat onto a different course as the approaching boat drew steadily closer. In it were four men. The pilot, a tall, massive fellow, was unmistakably Vordo. He was steering directly toward the boys' boat.

"They've seen us!" Joe cried.

Frank attempted some evasive maneuvers, while still heading for the mainland. But the other boat was faster. Although Frank spun his wheel sharply in a series of turns to port and starboard, their pursuers continued to gain.

Finally Vordo bore down, but as he did, Frank pointed skyward and yelled, "Look up there!"

Jack roared down in a screaming dive and pulled out directly in front of the powerboat. Then, just as a collision seemed imminent, Jack pulled up, missing Vordo and his men by inches. Vordo veered out of the way but Jack repeated his maneuver.

The Hardys and Chet momentarily forgot their predicament as they admired Jack's flying skill. At times he came so close to the surface that little water spouts were generated by the whirling propellers.

"Wow!" chortled Chet. "Vordo's getting discouraged."

"I'd say he's scared to death—and who wouldn't be. Attaboy, Jack!" Joe grinned.

Again and again Jack Wayne made close passes at the powerboat, forcing Vordo and his cohorts farther away from the boys. By the time the three sleuths neared the mainland, their pursuers were lost from sight. Jack then flew high above the boys, waggling his wings in salute.

Upon reaching shore, the Hardys turned Burly Wilkes over to the authorities. A police helicopter was immediately dispatched to the islet. Soon a report was radioed in from the copter. The island was deserted, and a search of the surrounding area had revealed no clues to the suspects.

Frank asked an officer if he might make a phone call to Ty Carter's airfield. Moments later he had Jack Wayne on the wire.

"Thanks for getting us out of this one," Frank said. "That was great flying."

The pilot chuckled. "I don't mind a little exercise now and then."

"Did you notice where Vordo was headed?"

"They took a northerly course, but I couldn't trail them because my fuel ran low. Sorry. I did give the police the lead."

Frank asked Jack to meet them at the hotel. "We'll stay at least another day, in case something turns up. Better bring the car you rented."

Next morning the Hardys received a telephone call from Ty Carter. He said a helioplane had just landed at his field.

"What's the registration number?" Frank asked excitedly.

When Carter told him, Frank noted that it was identical with that of the helioplane they had chased.

"I don't think it'll be staying here long," the man continued. "The pilot is sitting in the cockpit. Apparently he expects some passengers to show up any minute."

"Can you delay their take-off for a while?" Frank asked.

"I don't know. The guy seems to be in a great hurry. But I'll try."

Jack Wayne and the boys drove to the airport immediately and ran to the operations shack.

"They're taxiing out for take-off right now," Carter told them. He pointed through the window at the helioplane as it moved slowly toward the active runway. "I couldn't delay them any longer. The pilot asked that his plane be refueled. I told my line boys to take their time about it. But the pilot's passengers arrived."

"Vordo and his gang!" Joe exploded.

"Let's head them off!" Frank urged.

The boys dashed to their car and drove out after the taxiing aircraft. Moments later the car came to an abrupt halt, bogged down in a stretch of marshy ground just off the airport taxiway.

"Oh nuts!" Chet blurted.

"They're getting away!" Joe shouted.

Frank jumped out and chased after the helioplane. His companions followed. He was the first to reach the craft, just as it lined up for take-off. He recognized three of the passengers—Vordo, Bleeker, and the steward Timken. Frank lunged at the plane, but stumbled, lost his balance, and fell across the tail. The aircraft was moving so fast he could not let go.

Joe, Chet, and Jack, who had continued the chase, now stopped in their tracks and watched in horror.

The plane continued its take-off run, with Frank clinging desperately to the tail!

CHAPTER XI

Important Assignment

FRANK fought back panic as the helioplane lifted off the runway. With both hands he grabbed hold of one of the elevators and hoisted his body farther onto the tail.

He could feel the pilot tugging at the control wheel, but Frank's desperate hold on the elevator kept it from moving. The pilot was forced to reduce engine power and drop back down onto the ground.

He jammed the brakes on hard, then executed a partial ground-loop to avoid going off the end of the runway. The movement flung Frank from the tail onto the grass-covered shoulder.

Getting to his feet, dazed but unhurt, he watched helplessly as the plane headed down the runway. In a moment it had left the ground and was soaring upward.

"Quick!" Frank shouted as he ran to meet

Jack Wayne and the others. "Let's follow them!"

"You okay?" Joe asked.

When Frank said Yes, the four pursuers leaped into the Hardy plane and quickly took off. Ahead, Joe caught a glimpse of reflected sunlight flashing from the helioplane's metal wings.

"There it is!" he yelled.

Jack rammed the throttle ahead as far as it would go. He climbed rapidly above the altitude of the fugitives, then dived to get extra airspeed. The maneuver began to close the distance between the two craft.

"We're gaining on it!" Joe observed.

Chet pointed to the right wing of their own plane. "Look!" he yelled. "The fuel cap is loose!"

"On the left wing, too!" Joe shouted. By now both caps were vibrating furiously.

"That can't be," Jack Wayne insisted. "I checked them myself after I refueled!"

"This must be Vordo's doing!" Frank surmised.

The next moment the two caps came loose and fluttered in the wind on the small chains which held them to the tanks. Instantly the slipstream began to drag fuel from the wings. As two gossamer-like columns sailed off into the distance behind them, Jack Wayne applied hard aileron and rudder and turned back to the airport.

"I'm landing!" he said. "We're losing every

drop of gas. I just hope a spark from the engine exhaust doesn't ignite that trail of fuel, or we're goners!"

Tensely the boys watched gallon after gallon of high octane spray from the open tanks.

"How long will she keep running?" Frank asked anxiously.

"I don't know!" Jack replied. "But by the look of our fuel gauges—not long!"

Finally the airport came into view. Jack entered the traffic pattern just as their tanks ran dry. Starved of fuel, the engines sputtered, then quit completely. Fortunately, the plane was high enough to glide safely to the field.

"Whew!" Chet murmured as the wheels touched down lightly. "That's the closest I've ever come to being barbecued."

Jack grinned. "I was once told that flying involves long hours of boredom, interrupted by moments of extreme fright." He took a deep breath. "This was one of those moments."

"No use trying to go back up after the helioplane," Frank said disconsolately.

He telephoned Kenneth Dell at Great Circle Airways and told him of Burly Wilkes' capture and their father's escape.

"I learned about it yesterday," Dell replied. "In fact, your father was in contact with me."

"What!" Frank said excitedly. "You talked to Dad?"

"Yes. I would have told you sooner, but I didn't know where to get in touch."

"But he escaped over five days ago," Frank said. "Why didn't he let us know? Is he okay?"

"He's fine," Dell assured him. "However, I don't know where he is. He wants his whereabouts kept secret. Said he'd explain everything later and asked me to inform your mother, which I did."

Dell added that he had an important assignment for the boys, and would like to meet them at their home in Bayport the next day.

"Thanks," Frank said. "See you tomorrow."

Mrs. Hardy and Aunt Gertrude were overjoyed to see Frank and Joe that evening. But they were worried that Mr. Hardy was keeping his whereabouts a mystery.

"He's probably traveling incognito and in disguise," Aunt Gertrude said.

Thoroughly exhausted by their recent adventures, the boys went to bed shortly after dinner. The next morning they enjoyed a hearty breakfast of wheatcakes and sausages, then adjourned to their father's study. Kenneth Dell arrived shortly and joined the boys in the upstairs room.

"Well, I suppose you want to hear the assignment?" he asked, smiling.

"Yes," the boys replied, and Frank added, "What's your plan for us, Mr. Dell?"

"How would you like to fly to Scotland?"

The query caught the young detectives by surprise. "Scotland?" Joe echoed incredulously.

"That's right." Dell rose from his chair and began to pace the floor slowly.

"Two days ago I called Scotland Yard. They told me there have been several remarkably clever jewel thefts lately in Scotland. Each of them occurred on a day when the steward Timken was over there. The Yard checked and learned that he had visited Hexton's castle on those days.

"So we were right," said Frank "He is one of the gang."

"Yes, but as usual there is no usable evidence."

"If only Frank and I could get inside that castle," said Joe, "we could get the goods on both the UGLI operation and the robbery ring."

"That's exactly the idea," said Dell. "My airline is cooperating with the Scottish police and Inspector Clyde of Scotland Yard. I want you to go over as my operatives."

"We'd sure like to take a crack at it!" Frank declared.

"What about SKOOL?" Joe asked.

Dell shook his head. "No sale. They're going straight for Hexton himself and they're sure he's not at the castle just now."

"Have the authorities over there made any progress on the thefts?" Joe questioned.

"So far, they haven't turned up any evidence incriminating Hexton. One police official there will be working with you—Inspector Clyde. He's a member of the London Metropolitan Police—that's Scotland Yard, you know."

The boys nodded.

"Clyde is on special assignment in Scotland to see what he can dig up on our magician friend."

"When do you want us to leave?" Frank asked.

"One of our planes departs day after tomorrow."

"We'll be ready!" Frank promised.

"And by the way," the security chief added, "if you'd like to bring your friend Chet—"

"A herd of elephants couldn't stop him from coming!" Joe put in.

Dell said he would meet the boys at the Great Circle base for a final briefing the day of the flight. He then wished them luck and left.

Brimming with excitement, Joe phoned the news to Chet. "A castle in Scotland!" their chum exclaimed. "Wow!"

"Maybe we can find another magic silver bowl for you," Joe said jokingly. "One that works."

"Aw, come on," Chet protested. Then he perked up. "But wait till you see some of my new tricks!"

"We'll see them when we get back," Frank advised him. "Right now we'd better think about packing."

"You fellows just don't have any appreciation of my uncanny skill," Chet said and hung up.

Mrs. Hardy's and Aunt Gertrude's reactions to the coming trip were quite different. "Scotland!" the boys' aunt exclaimed. "First your father decides to play hide-and-seek, now you two want to go traipsing into danger on the other side of the Atlantic!"

Mrs. Hardy looked at her sons with a worried smile. "You know you have my permission. Just promise me you'll be careful."

"Of course we will," Frank and Joe assured her.

After supper they began preparations for their trip. Frank had just brought suitcases from the attic when the phone rang. He picked up the receiver.

"Are you Frank Hardy?" a man asked.

"That's right."

"I've got to see you." There was a note of urgency in the caller's voice. "It's important."

"First, suppose you tell me who you are," Frank said.

"I'm Stan Mazer, pilot of the helioplane!" was the astounding answer.

CHAPTER XII

A Startling Welcome

AMAZED and perplexed by the call, the Hardys agreed to meet the helioplane pilot the following day at their home.

"Why should he want to come here?" Joe asked. "If he's an UGLI agent, you'd think this is the last place he'd visit."

"It's sure strange," Frank agreed. "I can't wait to hear what he has to say. In any case, I think we should notify Dell to have him followed when he leaves here."

"Right." Joe telephoned the SKOOL man.

Late the following morning Stan Mazer arrived at the Hardy home. He was a middle-aged man, of medium height and slender build, and had a troubled expression.

"I'm Mazer," he announced.

The Hardys led him into the living room and they all sat down.

"You're the pilot of Hexton's helioplane?" Frank asked.

"That's right," Mazer answered. "I was hired about two months ago." He shifted nervously in his chair. "I needed a job so badly I snapped it up without question. But I didn't know it was connected with anything illegal."

"Weren't you ever suspicious?" Joe asked.

"Yes, from time to time, but I wasn't sure. Actually I closed my mind to the whole situation until you tried to stop my take-off."

"It was a pretty unnerving experience," Frank said dryly.

Mazer apologized. "I didn't know you were clinging to the tail until you were thrown clear," he explained. "I wanted to get out and help you, but Vordo forced me to take off."

"What about the day we chased you and Timken?" Joe said. "You turned right into us. We nearly collided!"

"I didn't know that was you," Mazer said, surprised. "I thought it was some hot-shot pilot wanting to play games. I pulled that maneuver hoping I'd throw a scare into him. Sorry."

When Frank asked Mazer where he had taken Vordo and his cohorts, the pilot replied, "To a large airport near New York City. When we landed, Vordo and his companions deplaned and disappeared—I had no idea where."

Mazer said that while he was parking the helioplane, he was confronted by a Federal agent, who told him that all FAA offices had been alerted to be on the lookout for the aircraft. To his surprise, the registration papers turned out to have been obtained under a fictitious name and address.

"The agent immediately impounded the plane," Mazer said, "and my pilot's license was revoked pending a hearing."

The Hardys asked him if he knew anything about their father's being kidnapped.

"I know nothing about that," he insisted, "although I did suspect something strange was going on in the lighthouse."

"In what way?" Joe asked.

"I was never allowed to enter," the pilot answered, "or even to remain long on the islet after delivering my passengers."

Frank pretended to be suspicious of the story. "Are you going to tell us you don't belong to the same secret criminal organization Hexton does? He wouldn't let you work for him if you didn't."

"What do you mean?" Mazer asked, and his amazement seemed genuine. "I never heard about any criminal organization and I'm certainly not a member!"

Joe asked him, "How did you learn who we are, and where to contact us?"

"Vordo mentioned your names during my last

flight," Mazer replied. "He said you're smart detectives."

Frank looked at the pilot searchingly. "What made you decide to come here and tell us all this?"

Mazer appeared harried. "After what happened at the airport, I knew I'd become involved in something that would get me into deep trouble," he confessed. "I thought if I told you fellows what I know, you'd help me."

Frank and Joe sensed that the pilot was being honest, and a slight nod between them said, "He's okay." They promised to do what they could and advised Mazer to repeat his story to Kenneth Dell.

"I'll do it at once," he said.

When the pilot left, the boys chuckled at the thought of the agent who had been assigned to follow Mazer. "I'd like to see his face when he tails him to Dell's office," said Joe.

The Hardys spent the rest of the day packing. Their flight to the Great Circle base was scheduled for the following morning.

Late that afternoon Chet's bright-yellow jalopy screeched to a halt in front of the Hardy home and the chubby youth leaped out.

"I'm packed and champing at the bit!" he exclaimed as he greeted his friends.

"Good!" Frank said. "How about dinner? Aunt Gertrude's trying out a new recipe for beef stew."

"Well—okay, but I'll have to make it fast. I want to get home in time for supper!"

Chet then assumed a nonchalant air. Strolling slowly around the room, he began to whistle softly. The boys watched as he extended his arms in front of him, then clenched his left hand into a fist. From it, with his right hand, he drew out a vivid purple silk scarf, followed by a train of varicolored kerchiefs.

"Bravo!" Joe said, clapping loudly.

"Great trick, eh? I thought you'd like it."

When the last scarf refused to come out, however, Chet became aggravated. "What's the matter with this thing?" He tugged on it violently.

"Something go wrong?" Joe needled.

Suddenly the kerchief pulled free and dragged the lining of Chet's jacket sleeve along with it. A small black container was revealed. From it popped a metal spring which shot through the air, then bounced around the floor like a grasshopper.

"So that's where all those scarfs came from," Frank said. He tried not to laugh.

Chet whipped off his jacket and frantically stuffed the lining back into the sleeve. As he chased the bouncing spring around the room, the Hardys burst into howls of laughter.

"You fellows are a jinx when it comes to my magic tricks," Chet said indignantly.

"Maybe Hexton will give you a few pointers when we get to his castle," Joe teased.

By the time Mrs. Hardy and Aunt Gertrude announced dinner, Chet had regained his composure. He had a second helping of dessert, then decided he must leave.

"Thanks for the delicious meal," he said.

Chet slowly rose from the dinner table. He stuffed the string of silk kerchiefs into his pocket and lumbered out to his jalopy.

The next day Frank and Joe said good-by to their mother and Aunt Gertrude, then drove off. They picked up Chet and went directly to the Bayport field. Jack Wayne was already warming up the engines when they arrived.

Tossing their luggage into the plane's baggage compartment, the boys climbed aboard and strapped themselves into their seats. Minutes later they were streaking down the runway on take-off.

Kenneth Dell was waiting for them at Great Circle's base. He gave a long briefing, then at six P.M. led the boys to the plane that was to whisk them overnight to Scotland. Chet and the Hardys took their seats with the other passengers. Soon the sleek jetliner roared down the runway, lifted off, and headed over the Atlantic.

After a while Chet struck up a conversation with a pretty red-haired stewardess. She managed to keep him amply supplied with food, while he related stories of his long and daring hours in the air.

"I don't like to boast," Chet said as he munched on a plateful of cookies, "but I'm going to wake up some morning and find I've sprouted wings if I don't spend more time on the ground."

Frank and Joe, meanwhile, studied every passenger aboard, occasionally strolling up and down the aisle on the chance they might recognize some member of Hexton's gang. But nothing seemed to be amiss. Also, no one indicated to the Hardys that he was a SKOOL man.

Suddenly the loudspeaker crackled to life. "This is your captain speaking," announced a deep voice. "We expect to encounter a cold front in a few minutes. The weather forecast lists it as a weak system, so there should be only light to moderate turbulence. We should be through most of it in forty minutes. Please fasten your seat belts and relax."

The boys looked out the window. Already the blue sky was beginning to be obscured by wisps of gray clouds. It grew so dark that the cabin lights had to be turned on. The jetliner began to toss jerkily. Chet fell quiet as the stewardess returned to her seat. He stared straight ahead with a blank expression.

"What's wrong with you?" Frank called across the aisle.

"I—I feel awful," Chet moaned. Seeing the stout boy's expression, the Hardys knew he had overeaten.

Chet remained tight-lipped for nearly fifty minutes until the plane came out of the churning clouds and into clear air. By this time he was asleep.

Several hours later the captain announced that the plane was commencing a gradual descent to Prestwick Airport, Scotland. For a moment the jetliner was enveloped in a milky whiteness as it entered a blanket of stratus clouds that stretched for miles north of the Irish Sea.

Frank looked down while the plane descended through the overcast. "That chain of islands over there must be the Hebrides," he said.

"And look!" Joe added, pointing off in the distance. "There's Ireland."

Suddenly Chet snapped alert. "Wh-where are we?" he asked.

"Just coming up on the Scottish coast," Joe told him. "How do you feel?"

Chet rubbed his eyes. "Oh—okay, I guess," he answered sleepily. "But never again so much food!"

"Oh no?" Joe grinned.

At seven o'clock Greenwich time, the jetliner's wheels touched down on the macadam surface of the runway and taxied to the parking ramp.

As the boys walked across the ramp toward the

administration building, a shiny black car marked "Police" sped up to them. Seated behind the wheel was a man with a large sweeping mustache and a hat pulled low over his eyes. He rolled down the window and called out, "Are you the Hardys?"

"That's right," Frank answered. "And our friend Chet Morton."

"Inspector Clyde sent me to fetch you chaps. He wants to see you right off. We'll send for your luggage later."

"What about customs?" Frank inquired.

"We've already arranged special clearance," the driver explained.

Frank, Joe, and Chet squeezed into the back seat. On the floor in front a blanket covered a large package. The car started off with a violent lurch. It sped across the airport ramp, out through an exit, and onto a road leading away from the field.

At that moment the driver yanked off the blanket. A man crouched beneath it straightened up and settled in his seat. The boys were flabbergasted at his sudden appearance.

"Wh-what—?" Frank started to say, when the man turned around and faced them. They gasped.

Vordo!

CHAPTER XIII

Sky Spies

As the boys stared in dismay, the driver pulled off his false mustache and removed his hat. Stony Bleeker!

Vordo looked at the Hardys with contempt. "Insist on poking your noses into our business, hey?" he growled. "We'll fix you for good!"

Frank realized that the boys could not risk attacking their abductors. The driver would surely lose control of the car and all might be killed. Besides, the men undoubtedly were armed.

Frantically the Hardys searched for a way out of their dilemma. Frank noticed that Bleeker was beginning to drift to the right.

Vordo also saw what was happening. "Get over to the left!" he snapped. "You know they drive on the opposite side of the road here!"

Bleeker swerved the car sharply to correct his

mistake. "Sorry," he said, mopping his forehead. "I keep forgetting we're not in the U.S."

"See that you don't forget again," Vordo growled, "or the Hardys and their fat friend won't be the only ones to regret this ride!"

Farther along, the road bent sharply in a hairpin curve. As Bleeker rounded it, he again instinctively favored the right side.

"Get over, you idiot!" Vordo bellowed, seeing a double-decker bus coming head-on.

Bleeker spun the wheel and the car rocked violently. Then, with a splintering crash, it tumbled over on its side! Vordo and Bleeker were thrown clear.

The three boys scrambled dazedly from the vehicle. The bus had stopped a short distance down the road. Its driver and several passengers were running toward them.

"Are you lads all right?" shouted the driver.

"Yes!" Frank called out. He then ran around to the front of the car. "Our men! Where are they?"

One of the passengers pointed off into the distance. "I saw two men disappear over that dune as we ran from the bus."

The boys gave chase but found no sign of Hexton's henchmen.

"We've let Vordo and Bleeker slip through our fingers again!" Joe said in disgust.

"But we're free," Frank reminded him.

"And still in one piece," Chet observed.

He and the Hardys walked back to the bus. Frank asked the driver to notify the police. Before long, three constables arrived to take the boys' story and examine the car. They said it was a stock model, rigged up to look like a police car.

"Clever job," a constable remarked. "I can see how it fooled the airport police."

He drove the boys back to Prestwick, where they checked through customs. One of the officials, recognizing their names on the passenger manifest, said that an Inspector Clyde had telephoned him shortly before they had landed.

"You're to meet him at the chief constable's office in Ianburgh," he said. "A car has been sent to pick you up."

The boys thanked him and lugged their suitcases to the front of the terminal, where the car was waiting. This time the driver produced a card to identify himself and the boys got in.

The trip to Ianburgh took little more than an hour. The visitors were intrigued by the pleasant rolling countryside, dotted with stone and thatch-roofed cottages.

At the chief constable's office they were greeted by a tall, distinguished-looking man who introduced himself as Inspector Clyde of Scotland Yard.

"My dear chaps," he said crisply, "I am sorry you have had such a rough reception." He turned to a stocky man with bristly gray hair and mustache. "This is my colleague, Chief Constable Burns."

"I've had a report on your kidnapping, of course," said the constable as he shook hands. "It was a daring trick. I think this gang has the wind up."

"They're scared," Frank agreed. "And that makes them more dangerous. But it doesn't matter. Through Hexton we might be able to identify the other members of UGLI and break the whole organization. But first we must get the goods on Hexton."

"That we must," Clyde said grimly. "UGLI has secret eyes and ears in every country of the world."

Burns nodded. "The jewel robberies are big—and very cleverly done—but they are nothing compared to the international danger."

"Will you be in charge of the investigation in Scotland?" Frank asked the inspector.

"Not officially," Clyde replied. "I have been invited to cooperate with the Scottish authorities."

The chief constable smiled at the boys. "Scotland Yard is tops, you know. Local authorities are often pleased to have them lend a hand."

"There's something that has always puzzled me," Chet interrupted. "How come Scotland Yard isn't in Scotland?"

"Many years ago—in 1829 to be exact," the inspector explained, "a police station and office were set up in a private house at Number 4 White-hall Place in London. The rear of the house opened onto a court named Scotland Yard because it was part of the palace grounds where the kings and queens of Scotland lodged when they visited the English Court in medieval times."

Frank was eager to return to the case. "Inspector Clyde," he said, "Joe and Chet and I would like to try to get into Hexton's castle."

"Good boys," said Clyde. "Dell told me you suggested it."

"Where is the place?" Joe asked.

Chief Constable Burns unfolded a map on his desk and the boys leaned over to study it. "About one hundred miles north of Ianburgh." He put his blunt finger down on a spot. "There it is. A huge stone fortress, set deep within a private park surrounded by miles of high iron fence."

Joe grinned. "Sounds like fun, getting in."

"Actually," said Clyde, "since the gang have impersonated officers and attempted kidnapping, we have a right to go there and demand entrance. But it would be defeating our purpose."

Frank nodded. "Yes. Vordo and Bleeker have sounded the alarm by now. Besides, by the time you got through the gates and up to the castle, every bit of evidence would be well hidden."

"It'll have to be an undercover job," Joe agreed.

"Maybe we could start by spying on it from the air," Frank suggested.

"Capital idea!" the inspector said.

"I know exactly the man who can help you," said Burns. "Aaron McHugh. He's an excellent pilot."

The chief constable said McHugh flew in the vicinity of Hexton's castle on a charter to the Hebrides, so the sight of his plane in the area would not be likely to arouse the suspicion of the magician and his men.

After leaving the constable's office, the boys went to their hotel and registered, then had showers, food, and several hours of rest.

That afternoon they were introduced to Aaron McHugh, a middle-aged man with a jutting square jaw and a crop of wiry brown hair that sprang out from his head.

The pilot was unusual looking, but his plane, which he used to haul cargo, was even more so. The boys were surprised and amused to see a metal-covered, trimotored craft with unusually thick wings and a system of exposed control cables that stretched back to the tail. Although the craft appeared antiquated, McHugh assured them that it was as durable and reliable as the day it was built.

"My tin bird is no' ver' fast, lads," he explained, "but it's a splendid workhorse."

Frank decided that they should waste no time in getting their first look at Hexton's castle.

"Chet, Joe," he said, "got your binoculars and cameras?"

"Righto," Chet replied.

Joe grinned and slapped the leather case slung over his shoulder. It also contained the Hardys' high-power photographic equipment.

The trio climbed aboard the plane and sat down on the floor. McHugh fired up the three engines. The craft lumbered along during the initial take-off run, then began to bounce lightly across the rough turf runway.

Soon it lifted off the ground and started to climb slowly, like a tired bird. When McHugh felt he had sufficient altitude, he tapped the various instruments on the panel with his finger to make sure none of the dials were sticking and giving false indications.

"We have a wee bit of a headwind," he announced, "so it will take about an hour to reach our destination."

The boys enjoyed the flight as they gazed down at the craggy landscape of the Scottish coast. As McHugh had estimated, nearly an hour elapsed before he pointed ahead.

"There it is!"

He adjusted his course, then rolled the plane into a shallow bank to give the boys a better look.

Far below was the large stone castle. Its sturdy gray battlements were sharply defined from an altitude of three thousand feet.

"It must be centuries old," Joe observed.

"About the eleventh century," McHugh said.

Chet exclaimed, "It has a moat, too, just like in the history books, but there's no water!"

"Nowadays, with planes," said their pilot, "a moat of water isn't much protection."

Frank asked McHugh to circle the castle without getting too close. Using binoculars, they peered down. Frank observed that the castle was on high ground, without trees or shrubbery, and noted that it would be impossible to approach it on foot without being seen.

Joe extracted a camera, attached a telephoto lens, and clicked off one frame after another. Presently his viewer picked up two men on the castle wall.

"Oh—oh!" he exclaimed. "We'd better get out of here. I think we've been spotted."

McHugh turned the plane back toward Ianburgh. When the craft landed, the Hardys hurried to the police darkroom to develop their photographs. To their disappointment, the glare of the sun on the plane's window had obscured a clear view of the castle.

"Rotten luck!" Joe exclaimed.

"We'll take another crack at it," Frank said.

He suggested that in order to avoid arousing suspicion, this should be done during one of McHugh's regular charter flights.

"Tomorrow morning I'm taking a load of feed to the sheep raisers near Stornaway in the Hebrides," the pilot told them. "Come along."

Shortly after dawn, McHugh and the boys again boarded the plane. Its fuselage was crammed with feed bags, and the three passengers had to worm their way to separate spots near the windows. The pilot started the engines and taxied out for take-off.

Without warning, a man appeared from behind a stack of feed bags and darted for the passenger door. Frank grabbed him and uttered a cry of surprise when he recognized the intruder's face. Timken, the Great Circle's steward! UGLI spying again!

"Let me out!" Timken shouted frantically. "I want to get off! You hear me?"

"I'm not deaf," Frank said, pinioning the man against one of the sacks. "Why are you here?"

As he spoke, the plane lifted. "We're already airborne," Frank continued. "I wouldn't suggest your taking a walk just now!"

With a snarl, Timken thrust his feet against the cabin wall and broke Frank's grip. He grabbed a feed bag and threw it at the boy, knocking him to the floor. But Frank sprang up and leaped at his attacker. Timken threw a punch, which Frank ducked. He got off a hard counterblow, catching the man squarely on the chin. The steward fell, unconscious.

"Joe, Chet!" Frank called out over the roar of the engine. "Lookee here! We have company!"

The boys climbed over the sacks.

"Timken!" Joe cried as he gazed in amazement at the man on the floor.

"Right."

"What's he doing here?" Chet asked.

"I don't know," Frank answered. "But we'll sure find out when he comes to!"

They tied up their unexpected passenger, then tried to revive him. Several minutes elapsed before Timken regained consciousness. When he realized he was still in the plane, he became panic-stricken. "How long have we been in the air?" he screamed.

"Why do you want to know?" Frank retorted.

"Quick! Tell me!" The steward's face turned pale with fear.

Frank glanced at his watch. "Ten . . . maybe fifteen minutes."

"Let me out of here!" Timken screeched. "You've got to land this plane, or we'll all be killed! There's a bomb aboard!"

CHAPTER XIV

Nerves of Steel

"A BOMB!" Frank shouted frantically.

"That's right!" the steward cried.

"Where is it?" Frank demanded, shaking Timken violently.

"In the nacelle of the left engine! You can't reach it!"

Frank dashed to the pilot's compartment to tell McHugh, who looked out his window at the stretch of rocky coastline below. "I no' can land in this area, lad!" he said grimly.

"But we have only minutes!" Frank looked out at the cowled engine, located beneath the left wing. "There's just one thing to do!"

"What's that?" the pilot asked.

"Climb out on the strut and try to reach that engine nacelle. I'll do it."

"But I no' have any parachutes aboard," Mc-

Hugh told him. "The slipstream might pull ye off the strut!"

"I must take that chance," Frank declared, "or we're goners!"

He went back to Timken. Seizing the steward by his collar, Frank pulled him to his feet. "Exactly where in the engine nacelle did you place the bomb?" he demanded.

"I . . . I put it just inside the access door to the oil-filler cap!" Timken stammered. "But it's too late! There's nothing you can do!"

Frank grabbed a screwdriver from the pilot's tool kit and slipped it in a pocket. He asked Joe and Chet to help him kick out the window located directly above the strut leading to the left engine.

As the boys kicked with all their might, the window cracked in several places, then shattered and disappeared below. The thunderous roar of the slipstream echoed through the interior of the fuselage.

Frank squeezed his body out the window. Hooking his legs around the strut, he pushed himself away. The force of the slipstream felt like the hand of some vengeful giant trying to hurl him off into space.

Frank, crouching low, locked his arms about the strut. He then proceeded to shimmy, at a painfully slow rate, toward the engine nacelle. Drawing closer, he moved into the area of the propeller blast and the engine exhausts. The sound was deafening, and the fumes and heat stifled him. However, they made him insensitive to the fact that he was hanging thousands of feet above the ground. Once Frank almost lost his grip.

McHugh reduced power on the right engine in an effort to ease Frank's ordeal. Joe and Chet watched anxiously, their nerves stretched almost to the breaking point.

Frank tightened his grip on the strut with one hand. With the other he took out the screwdriver and reached for the Dzus fasteners which secured the small aluminum access door on the nacelle.

The wind lashed against his outstretched arm, but he continued to probe for the fasteners. Finally the door loosened. It popped open and flapped violently.

Frank reached in through the opening and desperately felt for the bomb. Nothing! He stretched his arm in farther, his efforts becoming more frantic as his strength began to ebb. Then his hand felt something cylindrical in shape and about the size of a flashlight. Frank locked his fingers around the object and slowly drew it out. There was a small timing device at one end, revealing that the bomb had only seconds to run!

Now to get rid of it!

Looking down, Frank saw that they were still flying over a desolate stretch of coast. He flung the bomb from him and watched it hurtle down and behind the plane. It was almost out of sight when a white-and-black puff of smoke appeared. Seconds later the faint, thudding sound of an explosion could be heard.

Frank slowly worked his way back to the window and with the help of Joe and Chet dragged himself inside. Exhausted, he slumped to the floor.

"Whew!" Joe exclaimed. "That was close!"

"You can say that again," Frank said shakily. "Another ten or twenty seconds and it would have taken searchers a year to pick up the pieces."

"That was a brave deed, lad!" McHugh shouted from the cockpit. "And I'm grateful to ye for saving my ship! Do you want to go back to Ianburgh with your prisoner?"

"No," Frank replied. "Let's continue with the flight as planned. Timken isn't going to give us any trouble."

The boys returned to Timken. Joe asked, "Who put you up to this?"

"I didn't want to plant the bomb in your plane," Timken muttered, "but Vordo . . ." The UGLI assistant stopped short. Obviously their prisoner was fearful of what might happen to him if he talked.

"And Vordo got his instructions from Hexton, didn't he?" Frank pressed.

Beads of perspiration oozed from the steward's

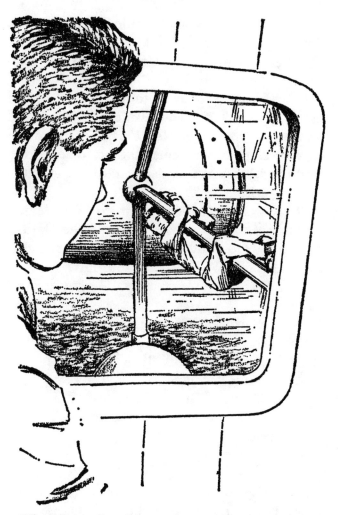

The pilot reduced power to ease Frank's ordeal

forehead. "I don't know! Vordo threatened me. I had to do it!"

"When did you and the others arrive in Scotland?" Joe questioned.

"The day after you tried to stop our take-off in the helioplane," Timken answered. "While we were at an airport near New York City, the plane was impounded by a Federal agent. When I told Vordo and Bleeker, they decided to get out of the country right away."

The steward's answer confirmed what Mazer, the pilot of the helioplane, had told the Hardys.

"Besides the pilot, there were four men that day," Joe said. "Who was the fourth?"

"One of Hexton's cronies. A guy named Arnold."

"Is he a spy for UGLI?" Frank snapped.

Timken jumped. "You know about—" The steward caught himself. "I won't talk to you lunks. I've said too much already!"

Joe spoke up. "Don't get so nasty, Timken. You forget that my brother saved your life. What kind of gratitude is this?"

Still no reply.

"Listen, buddy," Joe continued, "you know you're going to prison for trying to kill the rest of us. You might get a lighter sentence if you answer a few questions. For instance, what was your racket on the Great Circle flights?"

"I won't squeal!" Timken shouted, and clamped his lips together.

Joe shrugged. "Have it your way." The boys left their prisoner.

The plane landed at Stornaway and was quickly unloaded. After a conference, McHugh and the boys decided to return the UGLI agent to Ianburgh. On the return trip the pilot adjusted his course so the boys could take more aerial shots of Hexton's castle.

Back in Ianburgh, the Hardys handed their prisoner over to the chief constable, who was thunderstruck at the bomb story. He then let them develop their latest photographs. Frank spread the prints out on a table and they all scrutinized them closely. But the pictures revealed no clues.

"The ground around the castle is as clean as a whistle," Joe observed. "We couldn't possibly sneak up on the place without being seen."

"What about climbing up the surrounding wall?" Chet suggested. "Robin Hood used to do it all the time."

"Not a bad idea." Joe grinned. "But it brings us back to the original problem. How do we get inside the fence and up to the wall without being seen?"

Frank's brow creased in contemplation. "I'm afraid this is a tough one." He signed. "Whatever plan we come up with will have to be pretty far out."

At that moment Inspector Clyde arrived. He carried a long, slim black umbrella, which he hooked to the coat rack when he entered the room.

"Ah, there you are," the inspector said. "I have some interesting news for you chaps. Mr. Dell telephoned from the States while you were gone. He's leaving for Scotland immediately. Something very important and highly secret has come up!"

CHAPTER XV

A Furious Scot

DELL arrived in Ianburgh that same night and met the boys at the chief constable's office. There Inspector Clyde ushered them into the interrogation room and the young sleuths told about the capture of Timken.

"Great work!" the security chief exclaimed. "I'll want to question him myself before I go back to the States."

When Clyde left the room, Frank said, "I understand something important has come up on your end, too."

"Yes," Dell replied. "Our investigation has turned up a very interesting lead. Timken has been spending a lot of time with another Great Circle steward named Ross. We checked him out thoroughly and learned that he had a record for petty theft under another name. We suspect he's part of the Hexton–UGLI setup, but that he and Timken were working together."

"You mean they were double-crossing Hexton?" Joe asked.

"Yes. I doubt if Hexton would dispose of stolen goods in the clumsy way Timken has been doing."

"I see," said Frank. "These two manage to hold out a diamond here and there from the gang's robberies, then sell them."

"Right. We could pick Ross up on suspicion, of course. But I'd rather give him a little rope. Maybe we'll get a stronger case on him. Catching him first might make it easier to get Hexton."

"Where do we fit in?" Chet spoke up a bit fearfully.

Dell smiled. "Your assignment is to make a trip to the United States on our Flight 101. Ross will be steward. Use assumed names and occupations on the plane. Watch Ross and see if you can pick up any leads for SKOOL."

Joe grinned. "I'll feel like a secret agent on Flight 101!"

When Clyde returned, the Hardys told Dell about their aerial reconnaissance of Hexton's castle and of their efforts to think of some way to get inside.

The security chief laughed. "Sounds tough! But I'm betting on you." Dell told them that the next Flight 101 trip from Prestwick to New York was scheduled to depart in forty-eight hours.

"We'll have time to make another flight to the castle before we leave," Frank said. "I wonder if McHugh—"

Just then the telephone rang and the inspector picked up the receiver. "Hello. Inspector Clyde here! . . . Oh, it's you McHugh. . . . What? . . . Good heavens! That's incredible, I must say. Yes! The boys and I will start for the airport straight off!"

"What is it?" Frank asked.

"Somebody has cut the external control cables on McHugh's plane," he answered. "He wants to see us right away."

While Dell stayed behind, the inspector and the boys leaped into a police car and drove to the field. McHugh, in a furious mood, stood glowering beside his plane.

"Can you no' find the brigand who did this?" he shouted. "I'd like to get my hands on him! Here! Look at these!"

The boys examined the severed control cables, which dangled loosely from their connections at the tail and at the point where they entered the cockpit.

"Gee," Chet remarked, "they're cut clean in half."

"When did this happen?" Frank asked.

"It couldn't have been more than twenty minutes ago," McHugh replied. "While I was at the plane, I was told there was a telephone call for me in the office, so I went there. But no one was on the other end of the line. When I came back here, I found the cables cut!"

"Obviously the call was a trick to lure you away from your plane," Frank observed.

Just then there were sounds of a loud commotion in the airport office. McHugh hurried toward the building, followed by the others.

When they entered, an aircraft mechanic was clutching a stocky man by the arm. Another man, who McHugh said was the airport manager, was questioning the stranger.

"What's going on here?" Inspector Clyde demanded. "I'm with the chief constable's office!"

"I found this fellow going through my clothes locker," the mechanic said. "And look at what he was carrying!" He held up an oversized pair of scissors.

"Those are metal cutters," McHugh stormed. "So this is the brigand who cut my cables!"

"I didn't cut anything!" the man growled.

"Let me at him!" McHugh bellowed, and started to roll up his shirt sleeves.

"Calm yourself!" the inspector ordered. He turned to the man. "What were you doing at the locker?"

"It was open. I thought I'd look around. That's all!"

"What about these cutters?"

"I found 'em! Besides, is there any law against carrying metal cutters?"

The boys gazed at the man. There was something familiar about him, Frank thought, but he could not recall where he had seen him before.

Inspector Clyde demanded that the stranger show him some identification. The man hesitated. Then he pulled a wallet from his pocket and handed it to the inspector. It contained an international driver's license in the name of Karl Arnold.

"Arnold!" Frank exchanged a quick glance with Joe. "The man Timken said was the fourth passenger in the helioplane the day I tried to stop its take-off!" he said to himself. Aloud he exclaimed, "You're one of Hexton's men!"

"Hexton? Never heard of him," the man insisted.

"Don't lie to us!" Joe snapped. "We know who you are!"

"You've got me mixed up with somebody else," Arnold retorted with a smirk.

"Let me shake it out of him!" McHugh bellowed.

The boys urged the pilot to relax. Then they suggested that Arnold be taken back to the chief constable's office to have Timken identify him. The inspector agreed to do this.

Arnold seemed unconcerned as they returned to Ianburgh. When they reached the office, they found Dell questioning Timken in the interrogation room. The steward was visibly startled when he saw Arnold.

"We ran across one of your friends at the airport," Frank announced.

Timken was obviously nervous. "Friend?" he said shakily. "What friend?"

"This man right here," Frank replied sharply, pointing to Arnold.

"Why—I—I never saw him before," the steward insisted. "I don't know him."

"Stop playing games!" Joe ordered angrily. "This man is Karl Arnold. You told us about him!"

Arnold's face flushed with anger, but he said nothing.

"That was somebody else," Timken said. "I've never seen this man before."

"Satisfied?" Arnold said indignantly. "Now, if that's all, I'll leave!" He turned and stormed out of the room.

"But we can't let him go!" Joe protested.

"I'm afraid we must." The inspector sighed. "We haven't any evidence to hold him on, but we'll keep track of him."

"The inspector's right," Frank assured his brother. "We have no witnesses who saw him cut the control cables. And there is no law against carrying wire cutters. If he'd resisted the temptation to ransack the employees' lockers, he'd have got away altogether."

Dell looked discouraged as he and the boys left the interrogation room. "I didn't have much luck, either," he remarked. "Timken wouldn't tell me anything more than he told you."

"I suppose it's a pledge the UGLI men take," Frank said. "Besides, Timken is afraid of Hexton. That's why he wouldn't identify Arnold."

Minutes later, McHugh stalked into the chief constable's office. "I hope you have that Arnold fellow in jail!" he declared.

"We had to let him go," Frank admitted.

"What!" the pilot exclaimed. "Why, he's as guilty as a witch!"

"You don't have to tell us," Joe murmured.

"Can you repair the control cables?" Frank inquired.

"No," McHugh replied. "A new set will have to be made up special. It'll take two or three days before my tin bird will be flying again."

"Well," Frank said, "that washes out our plan for another reconnaissance flight before our trip. We'll have to wait until we get back."

The next day Dell, wishing the boys luck, returned to New York. The following morning the Hardys and Chet were on their way to Prestwick Airport, enthusiastic about their new assignment and the opportunity to spend a couple of days at home before returning to Scotland. Soon they were winging their way westbound across the Atlantic on Flight 101.

Frank was using the name Bud Richmond and introduced himself to a few passengers as an announcer on station WHOX, meaning to him HOAX.

Joe had chosen to be Larry Walker, a student returning from a hike through Scotland. Throughout the flight, both Hardys kept an eye on the steward Ross. Chet, as a pro-football player named Chuck Brown, spent most of his time in the galley getting lemonade and asking Ross a hundred unimportant questions.

He was always being interrupted by a whiskered old man wearing dark glasses, who was seated near the galley. From time to time both the steward and stewardess had to assure him that the wings were not bending off, that the engines were not about to catch fire, and they were sorry that the tea they had served was weak.

The only incident out of the ordinary occurred after landing at Great Circle's base. The elderly man accidentally tripped Ross with his cane while disembarking from the plane. The steward fell flat in the doorway and the old man leaned down to help him up.

"So sorry," he said in a high, quavering voice.

The boys had arranged to have Jack Wayne meet them, and after clearing customs, were soon on their way to Bayport. They were sorry not to have picked up any clues for SKOOL, but assumed Ross would be shadowed by agents.

The Hardys dropped Chet off at his farm, then drove quickly to their home. "Hello!" Mrs. Hardy cried out, and hugged her sons. "Did you see your dad?"

"No, Mother."

"He phoned a few minutes ago but didn't say where he's going. He's all right, though."

"Where did he phone from?" Joe asked.

"I don't know."

"You two boys look peaked," Aunt Gertrude spoke up, "but a few home-cooked meals will remedy that."

"It's good to be back," Frank declared.

The two women showed their disappointment when they heard that Frank and Joe would be returning to Scotland so soon.

"But we're sure eager for a shower and some American chow!" Joe said, grabbing the boys' two suitcases and bounding up the stairs. He set his bag on the bed and opened it to get a clean shirt.

"Hey! What's this?" he exclaimed, and picked up a carelessly hand-printed note from the top of his shirts. It read:

*YOUR FATHER WARNS BE CAREFUL.
GAME IS VERY DANGEROUS.*

CHAPTER XVI

Secret Compartment

"BUT who could have written this note and put it in your bag?" Frank exclaimed. "Didn't you lock it?"

"No, I never do." Joe looked at the message. "Maybe Hexton found out about our assignment, and had one of his UGLI men plant the note to throw us off the track."

Joe nodded. "And I bet I know when. At Prestwick the porter put our bags on his cart with a lot of other luggage, but then he went away for a while and the cart stood unattended."

Frank shrugged. "But what could Hexton possibly hope to gain? He knew it wouldn't stop us and we're aware it's dangerous."

Two days later Frank and Joe were again saying good-by to their mother and aunt. They picked up Chet at the Morton farm and headed

for the airport, where Jack was waiting to fly them
to the Great Circle base.

On the return trip to Scotland, the plane encountered moderate turbulence, but all the passengers took it calmly. The steward proved to be
Ross. When he saw them, the man at once became ill at ease.

After the boys took their seats, Joe whispered
to Frank, "I wonder if he suspects we're watching
him."

During the first half of the flight a blond-
haired man, wearing dark glasses, sideburns, a
small mustache and a beard, made his way down
the aisle several times.

"I have a feeling he's looking us over," Frank
said. "We'd better watch him as well as Ross."

Nothing suspicious happened during the flight,
however, and in the morning the jetliner landed
at Prestwick Airport. Frank and Joe made a point
of being the last passengers to leave. Chet was
just ahead.

While debarking, they all noticed that the
steward seemed in a hurry to leave the plane. He
ran down the steps after them and shot past.
Instantly the man in the dark glasses hurried toward the steward. Ross, seeing him, broke into a
run. The passenger sprinted ahead.

"Come on!" Frank exclaimed. "Let's see what's
up! It could be that passenger is a SKOOL man!
Maybe we can help him!"

The boys dashed after the two men, who disappeared around the corner of a hangar. Frank spotted the steward running into the building.

"Chet! Stay outside and cover the exits!" Frank cried. "Joe and I will go in after him!"

The building was filled with aircraft, which made it difficult for the Hardys to spot their quarry.

"Let's split up," Frank suggested. "I'll cover the left side, you take the right."

The boys separated. As Frank slowly wound his way among the aircraft, he heard a muffled noise and stopped to listen.

Bummf.

There it was again! The young sleuth's attention focused on a twin-engine plane directly ahead. Cautiously he stalked toward the cabin door. Just as Frank reached it, the door burst open and slammed into the boy's head with a force that made him cry out and sent him crashing to the floor. Half dazed, Frank looked up to see Ross leap from the craft and dart toward a side exit of the hangar.

"What's going on?" Joe called as he ran past the closely packed planes to his brother's side. "Are you all right?"

"I'm okay," Frank replied, getting slowly to his feet. "Just a little dizzy. Quick! Outside! Maybe Chet spotted Ross leaving the hangar!"

As the Hardys dashed from the building, they

saw Chet leaning against a low wire fence which enclosed an automobile parking lot. He was breathing hard.

"G-golly, but that guy could run!" the stout youth gasped as the Hardys approached him. He gulped in more air. "He's faster than a gazelle."

"You mean the steward?" Joe asked.

"Yes."

"Where did he go?" Frank queried.

"He jumped the fence into the parking lot and roared off in one of those little foreign sports cars," Chet answered. He stared at the ground with a sheepish expression, then began to shuffle some pebbles with his foot. "Sorry I goofed, fellows. I was checking the rear of the hangar when Ross zipped from the side exit. He had too much of a head start."

"That's okay," Frank said. "It would take a dozen men to cover a building that size."

"Hey! And something else!" Chet exclaimed, glancing up. "Just after you two chased inside after the steward, I caught a glimpse of that guy in the dark glasses watching from around a corner of the next hangar."

"Did you let on that you saw him?" Frank asked.

"Yes," his chum admitted. "In fact, I started walking toward him and he ducked behind the hangar. I thought of chasing him, but I didn't want to leave the exits unguarded."

"It's funny," said Frank. "He was chasing the steward, but apparently didn't try to catch him."

"That's not the only mystery," Joe added. "Chet, we wonder if that passenger is a secret agent from SKOOL. Let's try to find him and give a sign we're sort of working second hand for the organization."

"What kind of sign?" Chet asked.

"Oh, we could talk about school and school rings," Frank answered.

Chet was enthusiastic at once. "I'd feel a lot safer if I could hook up with a full-fledged SKOOL man."

The three boys made a thorough search of the place but failed to find the man. At last they gave up, went through customs, and took a taxi to Ianburgh. When they arrived, they found Inspector Clyde and the chief constable anxiously awaiting them.

"One of the constables was rechecking Timken's personal effects and he discovered a secret compartment in his wallet," the inspector explained. "Look what he found there—most extraordinary."

He handed an envelope to the young sleuths. Inside were a one-way train ticket to Edinburgh and a newspaper clipping. The item was headed:

Nairn Loch Manor to Be Opened to Public
Newly Discovered Jewel Collection on Display

"Nairn Loch Manor? Jewel collection? What's this about?" Joe asked.

"The Manor is to be maintained by the Scottish Trust as a historical shrine," Burns explained. "When they began to renovate it a few months ago, a worker discovered a magnificent collection of jewels hidden beneath the floor. It is said they were placed there about four hundred years ago."

"I remember reading about the discovery in a newspaper back home," Frank recalled. "The value of the collection is considered second only to the crown jewels in the Tower of London."

"Precisely," the inspector replied.

Joe looked at the clipping and train ticket again. "Do you think Hexton and his UGLI men might be planning to steal the collection?"

"I don't know," Inspector Clyde admitted. "We have to consider that possibility, of course. But the place will be so heavily guarded that any thieves will be caught."

"Why would Timken go to Edinburgh by train?" Joe asked. "I should think the thieves would use a car for a quick getaway."

"Most likely they will," Frank said. "Maybe Timken was only being sent there to case the place for Hexton."

"Exactly the conclusion I came to," Inspector Clyde declared. "Now they'll have to use someone else."

Joe snapped his fingers. "Perhaps that's where Ross was heading."

"We'll check," Clyde told him.

Frank was thoughtful for several seconds, then said, "Probably Hexton, with his sleight-of-hand ability, will do the actual stealing."

The conversation turned to the reason the boys had come to Scotland—to get into Hexton's castle.

Inspector Clyde paced the floor in thought. "The question remains, just how do you manage to do that?"

"Perhaps another reconnaissance flight will give us an idea," Frank suggested. "Let's alert McHugh."

"Oh!" Burns said quickly. "He isn't available at the moment. He's off ballooning."

"He's what?" Joe asked, with a puzzled expression.

"Ballooning," the chief constable repeated. "McHugh belongs to a club of enthusiasts who go darting about in bags filled with hot air. Jolly good fun, they think, unless they get caught in a tree, or on a church spire. They're having a race somewhere near Perth."

"What a ball!" Chet burst out. "I'd like to see that."

"Hold on!" Frank put in. "That solves our problem. We'll balloon into Hexton's castle!"

CHAPTER XVII

Night Attack

INSPECTOR Clyde laughed. "See here, my dear fellow. You're not serious about ballooning into Hexton's stronghold, are you?"

"I realize it sounds fantastic," Frank admitted. "But at least it's worth discussing with McHugh."

Joe scratched his head dubiously. "Hexton's guards are bound to spot a balloon."

"Maybe not if we drop in at night," Frank replied.

Chet pointed a determined finger at his friends. "Don't think you two are going to get me to ride in one of those oversized basketballs!"

Joe grinned. "Okay. Anyway, I don't believe there's enough hot air in Scotland to lift *you* off the ground!"

A little later the boys rented a car and drove to the site of the race. On a grassy plain a few miles west of Perth, more than fifty balloons of all shapes and sizes were preparing for the competitions. Their bright colors and vivid designs gave the scene a touch of the pageantry of a medieval tournament.

"Look at that!" Chet yelled as they walked across the field. He pointed to a balloon displaying the French national colors from its gondola. "What a beauty!"

At the firing of the starting gun, the contestants leaped onto bicycles, sped to their balloons, and jumped into the gondolas. Then the balloons were released from their moorings and sailed across the field. One of them never lifted off the ground; another, the French entry, rose into the air but became snagged in a tree branch.

"Nom d'une pipe!" screamed the flier. *"Il est fichu, mon beau ballon!"*

"Tough break," said Joe.

Frank asked one of the club members for McHugh. He learned that the pilot was not racing that day, but was helping another contestant a short distance down the field.

McHugh was surprised to see the boys. Frank told him about the plan for getting into Hexton's castle.

McHugh chuckled. "So ye want to be invaders?" he teased. " 'Tis a daring plan ye've come up with, lad. And it will no' be an easy thing to do."

"Can you get a balloon large enough to carry all of us?" Frank asked.

"Sure. We'll borrow one from the club."

"*I'm* not going," Chet insisted.

"But we need you for ballast," Joe said with a grin.

"If we get into Hexton's castle," Frank added, "you might see some of his magic equipment!"

"Well—" Chet muttered, weakening. "I guess you'll need somebody around to keep you two out of trouble."

After the races, McHugh and the boys returned to McHugh's apartment in Ianburgh to plan their daring adventure. The pilot examined an aeronautical chart and carefully plotted the position of the castle. He pointed out that their success depended entirely upon the winds and the position from which the balloon was launched.

"I understand a balloon has no directional control," Joe said.

"That's not entirely true," McHugh replied. "Since the wind direction generally changes with altitude, we can get some control by ascending or descending."

"How do you do that?" Chet questioned.

"By varying the amount of ballast, or weight carried in the form of sandbags," the pilot explained. "The more ballast dumped overboard, the higher the balloon will go. To descend, we simply release some of the gas from the bag by means of a valve."

"Just one thing," Joe put in. "If we manage

to reach Hexton's castle, how do we keep from floating right on past it?"

"By using a length of rope attached to a grapnel," Frank replied. "We'll lower it as we approach the castle—and hope it catches somewhere on the wall. This will act as a mooring. Then we can slide down the rope."

Chet took a deep gulp.

"Obviously," Frank continued, "we can't keep the balloon moored there. Hexton's men would spot it sooner or later. So, after we're down, we'll release the grapnel."

"Then I'll sail the balloon a short distance away and land," McHugh added. "With your approval, I'll ask one of the club members to help us. He can drive the lorry containing the launching equipment and assist in our take-off preparations. Later, he can rendezvous with me at the landing spot."

The boys thanked McHugh and drove back to Clyde's office.

"A report that will interest you chaps came in while you were gone," the inspector said. "An Ianburgh resident said he was involved in a minor automobile accident several hours ago. It happened on a road north of here. According to the report, it was a near head-on collision. Luckily, both drivers jammed on their brakes and merely smashed bumpers.

"This fellow stated that the other driver seemed in a devil of a hurry. He simply backed away and sped off in his sports car."

"Sports car!" Frank exclaimed. "Did the other driver get its license number?"

"Yes," the inspector replied. "I've checked it out. The car belongs to a chap named Ross."

"The steward we chased into the hangar!" Joe exclaimed.

"And another thing," Inspector Clyde said. "The accident occurred not far from Hexton's castle."

"I'm not surprised," Frank mused. "Ross could have been on his way there from Prestwick."

The boys were eager to get their balloon trip under way. Weather conditions the next night were unsuitable for the venture. But on the following night, McHugh telephoned the Hardys at their hotel room that, in his estimation, conditions were ideal.

"The way I calculate the winds, lads," he said, "we should take off from a point about five miles southeast of Hexton's castle. I'm familiar with the area, and know several open fields that will serve our purpose."

"Good!" Frank replied. "We'll meet you in a few minutes."

Frank relayed the message to the other boys and all checked the equipment they would take—

miniature tools, two-way radios, and pencil flashlights.

McHugh had telephoned his fellow club member and soon the lorry containing the balloon and launching equipment was at the door. McHugh was in his own car and the young sleuths hopped in with him. About two hours later the pilot pointed to a clearing just off the road.

"There's a good spot," he announced.

The boys helped to unload the balloon and set up the equipment to inflate it. Makeshift moorings were established to prevent the craft from floating away. Soon a large, spherical, gas-filled bag was looming over their heads, tugging gently at the mooring lines. McHugh and the boys climbed into the gondola and prepared to launch.

"Aye, the surface winds are very light," McHugh observed. "That'll make our attempt to moor at the castle much easier."

As they rose slowly into the air, Chet watched the ground slip away. "Hey!" he declared with a wide grin. "This isn't bad at all!"

A half moon in the night sky provided enough illumination for them to distinguish the terrain below. McHugh varied the altitude by dumping ballast and manipulating the gas-relief valve. The balloon altered its track slightly with changes in wind direction.

More than an hour passed, then Joe pointed directly ahead. "There it is!"

The medieval structure, turrets looming skyward, presented a ghostly image in the dim moonlight. As they drew near it, Chet called attention
to a far corner of the courtyard.

"Look!" he said. "A light! Seems to be coming
from one of the castle windows."

"No more loud talking," Frank ordered.
"We're getting close. Help me lower the grapnel
line over the side."

Slowly the balloon drifted toward the castle.
The pilot released gas and eased down to a lower
altitude. Just then a sharp, metallic sound pierced
the night air.

Ping!

"The grapnel just made contact with the castle
wall," Frank observed.

"What's that?" Chet whispered as he and the
Hardys heard a faint scraping sound.

Frank peered over the side of the gondola.
"The grapnel is being dragged up the side of the
wall," he murmured. "It isn't catching hold."

They floated over the courtyard toward the opposite wall. With a lurch the balloon came to a
halt.

"We've made it," Joe whispered excitedly.
"The grapnel caught."

"So far so good," Frank said tensely. "Now,
over the side and down the rope. I'll go first."

"Good luck, lad!" the pilot called.

The boys waited for a moment to make certain

the coast was clear. Then Frank eased himself over the side of the gondola and got a tight grip on the line. He hung precariously above the ground for an instant, then began to slide down.

Lowering himself gently onto the stone rampart, he peered through the darkness and listened. He then signaled for Joe and Chet to follow. When they were down, they freed the grapnel. The balloon drifted off into the darkness.

The three groped their way along, finally coming to a flight of stone steps. Frank cautiously led his companions down the stairs into the courtyard below.

"There's the light I spotted from the air," Chet whispered, pointing across the courtyard.

"And the door right next to it is partially open," Joe observed.

The boys crept forward slowly until they reached the door. Frank eased it open wider. Peering inside, they saw a long, dimly lighted corridor which extended deep into the castle. It was lined with suits of armor mounted on low, wheeled platforms.

"I don't see anybody around," Joe whispered. "Let's go in."

At intervals along the corridor were large wooden doors with massive iron hinges. As the young sleuths neared the end, they heard muffled voices coming from a room. Its door was slightly

ajar. Slowly they stalked toward it and Frank
looked inside.

*Clustered around a huge oak table were Hex-
ton, Vordo, Bleeker, Arnold, Ross, and the short
twins.*

Hexton's voice carried through the opening.
"Now get this straight, Vordo. You all know the
layout of Nairn Loch Manor?"

"Every detail," Vordo replied.

"No mistakes," Hexton said harshly. "You
especially, Bert and Lou." The twins nodded.

"Then it's all set," Hexton said. "Day after
tomorrow we'll have in our hands the most valuable collection of jewels in Scotland!"

Frank stiffened. So Hexton *did* plan to steal
the Nairn Loch collection before it went on display!

The men stood up to leave, their chairs scraping on the stone floor. Instantly Frank motioned
Joe and Chet to retreat down the corridor. Chet
hesitated before a suit of armor.

"What are you doing?" Joe whispered.

"Getting myself a weapon." Chet began to tug
at a mace.

A metal gauntlet pulled loose and crashed to
the stone floor. The sound echoed through the
corridor like a burst of thunder. The door
creaked open and the men sprang from the room.

"W-why, it's those snoopers!" Vordo bellowed
in surprise.

"Get them!" Hexton commanded.

When the men lunged at the trio, Joe caught Arnold with an uppercut that sent him spinning across the corridor. Frank pushed a suit of armor from its platform, directly into the path of the UGLI men.

"Watch out for Vordo!" he yelled at his brother.

Joe whirled to see Vordo picking up the gauntlet. He flung it at the young sleuth. The heavy object grazed Joe's head, stunning him.

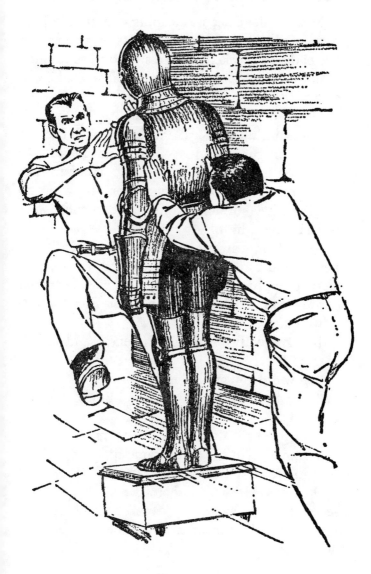

Meanwhile, Chet was leaping behind one platform after another, pushing suits of armor into the paths of Bleeker and Ross, who were lunging at him. The stout youth grabbed a lance and charged the men.

"Look out!" Bleeker howled.

Chet continued his gallant charge, with Bleeker and Ross running just inches ahead of the point. But the lance proved too cumbersome. The tip lowered to the stone floor, throwing up sparks. Chet stumbled and the two men were quickly upon him.

Arnold, meanwhile, recovered from Joe's uppercut and ran to help Hexton and Vordo, who were grappling with Frank. Three adversaries proved too much and Frank was finally overpowered.

Joe gradually regained his senses and scrambled to his feet. Hexton glared at them.

"How did you get in here?"

"Figure that out for yourself!" Frank snapped defiantly.

"What now?" Vordo asked Hexton.

The magician's decision came quickly. "We've no time to waste," he said. "Let's take these sons of Fenton Hardy and their friend through the secret passageway to my storeroom. We'll keep them around as insurance—in case we run into any trouble."

"I'll go ahead and open the door," Bleeker volunteered.

The boys were frisked and the tool kits were removed from the secret pockets of their jackets. Their miniature short-wave radios were also taken.

"Leave 'em their flashlights," Hexton said, and added with a sardonic chuckle, "It'll help 'em see what a lot of trouble they got themselves into."

The three prisoners were prodded along the corridor, then through a camouflaged opening in the wall. Single file, they walked down a long, stone staircase and through a secret passage beyond. The boys could see nothing of their surroundings other than what Vordo's flashlight picked out of the darkness, but they felt a clammy dampness in the air.

"Here we are," Hexton said finally.

Directly ahead was a huge iron door. The hinges squeaked as Vordo pulled it open.

"Get in there!" Bleeker growled.

The Hardys and Chet were shoved into a large dungeon-like room. Scattered about were various devices that Hexton had developed for his magic shows.

"We can't keep 'em here!" Vordo warned. "The lock on this door is so old it won't work!"

"I know," Hexton replied. "But I've something else in mind."

He pointed to an oversized trunk, standing on end. It was constructed entirely of heavy steel, and held together with large rivets. Near the base were several air holes.

Hexton removed the three massive padlocks that secured the trunk. "Put them in here," he ordered. "They'll never escape from this!"

"You can't do that!" Joe shouted. "There isn't enough room!"

"Shut up!" Vordo snarled.

The magician's cohorts pushed the boys toward the trunk and forced them to step inside.

"This will give you time to regret that you ever thought you could outsmart the Incredible Hexton!" the magician declared, uttering a spine-chilling laugh.

Seconds later the trunk was slammed shut, and the Hardys and Chet were locked in inky black-ness!

CHAPTER XVIII

Chet's Big Assist

"WE'LL never break out of here!" Chet told the Hardys.

"It does look pretty hopeless," Joe admitted glumly.

"Think!" Frank commanded. "We have to come up with something!"

He and the others took the pencil flashlights from their pockets and played the beams around the small steel prison. They saw no chance of escape.

"Hexton was right," Frank conceded gloomily.

"Hey!" Chet burst out. "Turn your flashlights this way."

He began to explore the top and sides of their enclosure. Finally he said, "Hmm. There might be a way out of here—"

"No kidding," Joe declared. "In case you're

thinking of a magic trick to make us fit through the keyhole, forget it."

"Nothing short of an acetylene torch can solve our problem," Frank put in. "These trunk walls must be an inch thick."

"I know," Chet said, "but look at those rivets."

"What about them?"

"The ones along the top," Chet explained, "are just a bit shinier than those along the sides."

The Hardys nodded in agreement.

"Do one of you have a pocketknife?" Chet asked. "Or did the UGLI's take it?"

"That's something they missed," Frank answered. "Here."

He and Joe looked on quizzically as Chet placed the point of the blade against the edge of a rivet at the top of the trunk. Clenching his fist, he hammered against the end of the knife. After several sharp blows, the rivet turned slightly.

"Eureka!" Chet shouted. "I was right!"

"How about letting us in on whatever you've found?" Joe pleaded impatiently.

"The top of this overgrown trunk," Chet explained, "is attached by false rivets."

"False rivets?" Frank queried.

"Yes," his chum replied. "Actually they're not solid rivets, but are cut through in the middle and threaded so the ends can be screwed together just like a regular nut and bolt."

The Hardys looked at Chet in amazement.

"How did you happen to know about this?" Frank asked.

"When I began to study magic," Chet replied, "I read a book about famous magicians. A few, like Houdini, were also great escape artists. The book described false rivets as one of the tricks they used."

Chet continued to pound his fist against the knife. Soon the rivet head was loose enough to turn by hand. After several twists, it came apart.

"This is the hard way of doing it," Chet said. "The escape artist uses a special wrench which fits over the rivet head. That's why these are shinier than the others."

"Boy, your interest in magic really paid off," Frank remarked with a grin.

"But why would Hexton lock us up in something we could escape from?" Joe asked.

"He never expected any of us to figure it out," Frank surmised.

By this time Chet had loosened three of the rivet heads. Frank and Joe each took a turn working with the knife. The job was hard and tedious. Several hours passed before the last of the false rivets was unfastened.

Grinning in satisfaction, the boys pushed up against the metal top. It broke free and toppled to the floor with a loud bang. Elated, they quickly scrambled out of the trunk and stretched their aching bodies.

"Great going, Chet," murmured Joe.

Frank echoed this, then beckoned the others to the door. The lock was, indeed, defective and the boys had no difficulty opening it. They stepped outside into a small vestibule. There they saw the entrances to several passageways.

"Leaping hyenas!" Joe exclaimed. "Which way do we go?"

"Golly!" Chet gasped. "Do you fellows remember which passage Hexton and his men brought us through?"

"I didn't realize there was more than one," Frank admitted. "It was too dark to see."

"This is like a maze." Joe shook his head in bewilderment.

Using his flashlight, Frank led the others through one of the passageways, up flights of stone steps, through places where the ceiling was so low that they almost had to crawl, then along several sharp turns that completely confused them.

"We're not getting anywhere," Chet complained.

"This castle must be honeycombed with secret corridors," Frank said.

He swept his flashlight beam ahead and saw that the passage branched off in three different directions. They went down the middle one for what seemed like an hour, but could only have been a few minutes. It came to an abrupt end. They were facing a blank wall.

"Now what?" Joe sighed.

"What I wouldn't give for a road map of this place!" Chet mumbled.

The boys backtracked, then turned down the left passageway. More stone steps led them deeper and deeper inside the cellar of the castle.

Presently Frank stopped short. "Wait a minute," he ordered. "Do you fellows notice anything?"

"Not me," Chet said.

"I don't— Say!" Joe replied. "The air is getting real damp and clammy!"

"Right," his brother agreed. "Just like it was in the passage to Hexton's storeroom. Maybe we're on the right track."

The boys continued on and made several sharp turns. Frank pointed his flashlight ahead and uttered a cry of dismay. They stood before the iron door to the storeroom, the very same place from which they had started!

At that moment they heard muffled footsteps. Frank snapped off his flash. From a distance, beams of light played across the iron door. The trio flattened themselves against the wall where it angled away from a little alcove.

Frank leaned closer to Joe and Chet. "It must be a couple of UGLI's to check on us," he whispered. "Watch where they come from. It'll have to be the passageway that will lead us out of here."

The men drew near. Would they see the escaped prisoners? Fortunately the men failed to notice the Hardys and Chet in the darkness and entered the storeroom.

"Hey!" came a shout almost immediately. "They're gone!"

By this time the boys had dashed down the corridor, along which the men had come.

"There they go!" one of Hexton's pals yelled. "After 'em!"

Frank, Joe, and Chet had a good head start. They ran as fast as the narrow, winding passageway would permit. Behind them swept the beams from the flashlights of their pursuers.

Ahead, the tunnel forked out into two flights of steps. "Oh no!" Joe cried despairingly. "Which way?"

Frank searched the steps with his flashlight. The ones on the left were more worn. "This way," he said as the sound of the pounding feet behind them grew louder.

The three boys raced up the long flight of steps and down another corridor, but soon realized that their choice was wrong. The passage ended in a blank wooden wall!

"There *must* be a way out!" Frank declared. He picked up a loose stone and hammered against the wall. "Listen!" he said. "This wall doesn't sound solid. It must have a secret panel. Quick! Help me get it open."

Joe and Chet pushed against the wall with all their strength.

"It won't budge!" Joe gasped.

The sounds of their pursuers' approach pounded in their ears. As the trio braced themselves for the oncoming struggle, there was a sudden grinding noise in the wall. They turned to see a panel slowly opening. A man, holding a flashlight, poked his head from behind the secret door. The boys' eyes widened in astonishment.

Kenneth Dell!

CHAPTER XIX

"*Prepare to Ditch!*"

"FRANK! Joe! Chet!" Great Circle's security chief exclaimed.

Behind him in a hallway stood Inspector Clyde. "I say!" he exclaimed. "What are you chaps doing in there?"

Before the three startled boys could reply, their pursuers rushed up. They almost collided as they came to an abrupt halt. Bug-eyed, Hexton's pals gazed at the lawmen, reinforced by other police. The UGLI's whirled about and ran back through the passageway.

"Come on!" Frank shouted. "After them!"

The boys rapidly gained on the men. Frank, in the lead, caught the nearest one with a flying tackle. He fell against the pair ahead, causing them to topple like a row of dominoes. There was a brief struggle while Inspector Clyde and several Scottish police officers rushed up to help the boys subdue their captives.

The UGLI men were handcuffed and led away by the police, while Frank, Joe, and Chet followed Dell and the inspector through the open panel into the main hall of the castle. They noticed it was already daylight, and Chet yawned sleepily as the group went to sit down in a huge library.

"We're amazed to see you, Mr. Dell—and you, Inspector," Frank said. "How did you get in without being caught?"

"First, let me tell you why I came here," Dell said. "SKOOL's work is paying off at last. Frank and Joe, your father has almost single-handedly cracked UGLI's operations in all European countries except the British Isles, and in the United States."

"That's great!" Frank exclaimed.

"It sure is," Joe added. "And the mystery of the undercover work here is—well, half solved."

Clyde said that shortly after dawn McHugh had telephoned him, fearful something must have happened to the boys. "I gathered a few constables together and came straight here."

"Lucky break for us!" Joe remarked.

"At the castle gate," Clyde continued, "we met a most unsavory-looking character. One of the constables recognized him as a thief wanted by the police in Glasgow. He resisted arrest and ran into the castle. We chased him."

Clyde told the boys that inside he and the constables had encountered four other men who also resisted arrest. They were Arnold, Ross, and the twins.

"I questioned them," he said, "but they refused to talk."

"What about Hexton, Vordo, and Bleeker?" Frank asked.

"Apparently all three got away," the inspector said. "Tell us, what happened to you?"

Joe briefed the men, then said, "I'll bet Hexton and the others are on their way to Edinburgh. Last night we overheard them discussing plans to steal the jewels at Nairn Loch Manor before it's opened to the pub—"

Joe stopped speaking at the sound of a faint hissing and turned abruptly. Then he burst out laughing and pointed to Chet, who had fallen asleep in an easy chair. His hands were folded on his stomach and he snored lightly.

"You all deserve a good sleep," Dell suggested, but the Hardys were too excited to accept the idea. There were still many questions to be asked.

"How did you find the entrance to the secret passageway?" Frank wanted to know.

Dell replied, "We were starting to search for you when a pounding sound came from the other side of the wall. All of us suspected it might be you signaling for help and hunted for a secret panel. I discovered that by moving the left gauntlet on one of the suits of armor in the main hall, a portion of the wall began to open!"

"And thank goodness," said Joe. "We thought that wall was the end of the line for us."

"Somewhere in this castle," Frank spoke up, "there must be evidence of Hexton's espionage setup. Have you found it?"

"No," Dell replied. "Haven't had time to look."

"Let's see if we can find it," Joe suggested.

No one had the heart to awaken Chet, so they left him. Inspector Clyde offered to investigate the library. Dell and the boys started down the adjoining hall to examine various other rooms.

The Hardys looked into several, but saw nothing to indicate espionage paraphernalia. At the end of the hall, they found themselves facing an enormous faded tapestry.

"Maybe this hides something," Frank said.

He and Joe slipped behind the hanging and found a large double door which opened inward. As they entered, the Hardys were awed by the vastness of the room. The ceiling arched high above their heads, and lancet windows spilled bright sunlight onto the floor. At one end was a huge map of the world with colored pins stuck in various cities.

"UGLI's centers of operation!" Frank exclaimed. "If Dad missed any, this will tell him where else to look!"

In the center of the room stood two oak tables. There was an elaborate radio setup on one. Joe whistled. "Powerful baby!"

On the other table were several metal cases, sealed without any visible means of opening.

"Trick boxes," said Frank. "One of Hexton's specialties."

Dell walked in as the boys looked them over and tried pressure in several places. Nothing worked. Then Frank had an idea. He turned one box toward him and the side slowly opened.

Joe grinned. "Hardy, the magician!"

"No," said Frank. "Electric eye." He moved the other two cases and each opened in the same way, revealing rows of drawers.

In the first one the boys found packages of microfilm and microtape, each labeled with a code tag.

"Tells where they came from and where they're going," Frank guessed. "Hexton brings them here. UGLI operators make the pickup and take them to countries hostile to the United States and other democratic powers."

Dell frowned. "These are probably films of secret plans and drawings of highly classified material."

"Here's the roster of UGLI operators!" Joe exclaimed, riffling through a notebook. "Probably these names are in code."

"Doesn't matter," said Frank. He held up a red leather volume. "Here's the codebook!"

"Well," said Inspector Clyde, entering the room, "that will come in handy when it's time to round up those UGLI blighters. I saw the tapestry hanging awry and guessed you might have found a hidden door."

He stood in amazement at the boys' discovery. "What a treasure for Scotland Yard, the FBI—"

"And SKOOL," Joe spoke up. "UGLI, the biggest undercover subversive operation in the world, cracked wide open!"

Frank's enthusiasm was dampened by the fact that some of UGLI's top men were still at large. "Unless we catch them, they'll start a new operation somewhere else."

"That's true," Clyde said, and the others agreed.

"Then let's find them!" Joe cried.

At that moment a constable ushered in McHugh.

"I returned to Ianburgh to get my plane," the pilot said, "and flew 'er back here. Thought I might be a wee bit o' help." He had landed on an open field close to the castle, he told them.

"That's great!" Frank replied eagerly. "Will you fly us to Edinburgh?"

"Certainly."

McHugh was introduced to Dell. The pilot grinned. "Man, ye got a couple o' fine detective lads here," he said. "Well, I'm ready to start."

Inspector Clyde decided to stay at the castle. "I'd better remain here in case something important pops up on this end."

Frank and Joe roused Chet, who rubbed his eyes and stubbornly demanded breakfast.

"Come on!" Joe urged. "We'll grab a bite when we land. Chet, wait till you hear what we found!"

This roused the stout boy and he followed the Hardys and Dell to the plane. All the boys cat-napped during the flight, and later at Edinburgh Airport stoked up on bacon and eggs. Then, while McHugh stayed with the plane, the boys and Dell went to the local police office to reveal Hexton's daring scheme of robbery the next day.

The constable on duty, a plump man with reddish hair who introduced himself as Officer Watson, was highly indignant. "Impossible! Thieves could not get within five hundred feet of the Manor without being challenged!"

"Don't underestimate Hexton," Dell warned. "He's an extremely clever crook."

"Now that he knows we're after him," said Frank, "he might very well pull the robbery to-day."

"Is Nairn Loch Manor far from here?" Joe inquired.

"Oh, just a few minutes by car," Watson replied.

"Will you come with us?" Dell asked him.

"Well—all right. But I tell you, this man Hexton hasn't got a chance!"

They climbed into Watson's car and soon arrived at the large, fortress-like structure built of stone. The windows were heavily barred, and the thick oak doors were secured by large iron bolts.

Watson showed his credentials, then introduced his companions. He asked to see the custodian, Angus Hamilton. The custodian scoffed when he heard about Hexton's intentions. "Impossible! Utterly impossible!" he asserted. "The Manor is too well guarded."

"What about burglar alarms?" Frank asked.

"A complete system is now being installed," Hamilton answered. "In fact, the Manor will not be opened to the public until it's completed." He grinned. "No, I'm afraid your fears are unwarranted. This Hexton fellow would have to render himself invisible to get onto the premises."

"I'm not sure he couldn't do just that," Chet mumbled.

"May we see the jewel collection?" Frank requested.

"I'll be happy to show it to you," Hamilton said with pride.

He led them down a long hallway. At the far end was a heavy oak door, flanked on each side by a guard. With a large black key the custodian unlocked the door. He ushered the Hardys and their companions into the chamber.

"You gentlemen," Hamilton said, "are about to see one of the most splendid collections of—" His voice trailed off, and his face turned ashen. "The jewels!" he gasped. "The jewels! They're gone!"

The Hardys ran to the glass cases in which the treasure had been kept. Except for a gold crown and several scepters, the cases were empty!

"B-but how?" the custodian cried, almost in a state of panic. "I checked the collection just a little while ago!"

The local constable took command of the situation and questioned the guards. None of them had seen any suspicious strangers in the area. A quick inventory revealed that all the smaller, but extremely valuable jewels were missing.

"Hexton left the crown and scepters behind because they're too bulky," Frank surmised.

"What's your guess, Mr. Dell," asked Joe, "as to the way the thieves got in here?"

Dell turned to the custodian. "Are there any architectural plans of the Manor available?"

"Indeed yes. I have them in my files. But if you're looking for a secret passageway, you won't have any luck. I've studied those plans thoroughly."

Watson, meanwhile, had telephoned his office and ordered his men to close off all roads leading out of Edinburgh. Also, airports and piers throughout the country would be alerted at once.

"Do you think Hexton is headed back to his castle?" Joe asked.

"If so," Frank said, "he'll find quite a welcoming committee waiting for him. But now that he knows the police were there, I'd say he'll stay away from the place."

"We'd better phone Inspector Clyde about the robbery," said Chet. But when Joe tried to do this, he found there was no telephone at the castle.

"We'd better fly back there right away," Frank said.

Dell announced he must return to the United States. "If Hexton comes there, I'll be on hand to pursue that part of my assignment." He said good-by and went off in a taxi.

Watson drove the boys to the airport, then went back to his office. As the young detectives hurried toward the trimotored plane, they saw that the pilot was already seated in the cockpit. Frank signaled to him and McHugh responded with a not-too-enthusiastic wave of his hand.

"Something seems to be troubling him," Joe

observed as they climbed into the cabin and slammed the door. The pilot started the engines and the plane began to taxi toward the runway for take-off.

Frank walked up to the cockpit. "What seems to be the mat—" He stopped abruptly and gasped. Crouched in the seat next to McHugh was Stony Bleeker! He held a gun pointed at the pilot.

"Get back into the cabin!" Bleeker commanded.

Frank turned to see two men emerge from beneath a tarpaulin at the rear. *Hexton and Yordo!*

"It's nice of you boys to accommodate us like this," the magician said with a smirk. "We happened to be in need of fast transportation."

"W-when did you get aboard?" Joe stammered. "We thought you'd be a long way from Edinburgh by this time!"

"Our car broke down on a back road near the airport," Hexton snapped. "Then Bleeker spotted this plane and we decided to hitch a ride."

"Where to?" Joe demanded.

"We're all going for a nice little flight to Ireland," the magician announced sarcastically.

"I told you I can no' make it there!" McHugh shouted. "We've no' enough fuel!"

"Don't try to fool me!" Bleeker growled. "Your gauges show full tanks!"

"The gauges haven't worked for weeks!" the pilot insisted. "I calculate my fuel consumption

by the amount of time I fly. And I tell ye, we no'
have enough fuel to make Ireland!"

Hexton let out a spine-chilling laugh, and eyed
the Hardys and Chet. "Your pilot will have to
think up a cleverer trick than that, because I don't
intend to go back to my castle and meet your
Inspector Clyde!"

"How do you know about that?" Frank asked.

The magician's weird, piercing eyes focused on
the boys with a fixed stare. "Bleeker stayed behind when Vordo and I left for Edinburgh," he
replied. "He was there when the constables
arrived, and escaped without being seen. Of
course he came straight to Edinburgh to warn
us."

"Incidentally," Frank put in, "how did you
manage to pull off the Manor robbery?"

"Shut up!" Vordo growled. "You're asking too
many questions!"

"No, no, Vordo. I don't mind telling them,"
Hexton said boastfully. He reached into his
jacket pocket and withdrew a folded piece of
parchment. "This," he said, "is the architect's
original plan of Nairn Loch Manor. There are
copies, of course. But this is the only one showing
the secret passageway."

"The passageway," Frank said, "that leads into
the chamber where the jewel collection was
kept."

"Yes, and very convenient for me," the magician replied smugly, "especially since its entrance is located in a hill nearly a quarter of a mile away. As for this," he added, tapping the parchment, "it used to be on display in a small private museum, but a master key and a little sleight of hand put it in my pocket."

As the plane continued on course, the Hardys noticed that their captors' jackets bulged and a sealskin pouch jutted from one of Hexton's pockets. Undoubtedly it contained the stolen jewels!

A few minutes later McHugh shouted another warning. "We're leavin' the coast! We can no' go any farther!"

Frank gazed below. They were passing over the west coast of Scotland and heading out over the Irish Sea. Just then the port engine sputtered. Seconds later the center and starboard engines began to quit.

McHugh whirled the plane in a tight turn back toward the Scottish coast. Leveling the craft out on a reciprocal course, he tightened his grip on the control wheel.

Frank and Joe stared at the propellers as they windmilled noiselessly in the powerless glide. Below them was the choppy surface of the Irish Sea.

"I can no' reach land!" McHugh shouted. "We're goin' down. Prepare to ditch!"

CHAPTER XX

Desperate Flight!

McHugh flicked his radio transmitter to 121.5 megacycles—the international distress frequency.

"Mayday! Mayday! Mayday!" he shouted into the microphone. "This is Trimotor—Victor—Victor—Fox! About twenty miles southwest o' Skipness radio! Lost all power! Have t' ditch!"

Hexton and his cohorts were pale with fright as they watched the plane sink closer to the water.

"Quick, lads! Jettison the cabin door!" McHugh ordered.

Near the door was a red handle. Joe dashed to it and gave a sharp pull. As the door shot off into space, there was a thunderous rush of air through the cabin.

"Sit with your backs against the forward bulkhead!" the pilot yelled. "Clasp your hands behind your heads and brace yourselves!"

Everyone took ditching positions. The wait was

nerve-shattering. Finally the plane hit the water. It bounced off the surface on first contact, then nosed down into the choppy sea with a violent impact. Water gushed into the cabin. As the boys recovered from the shock, Frank turned to see Hexton pushing himself out through the cabin entrance.

"We're sinking fast!" Joe yelled.

"Look!" Chet shouted. "McHugh's unconscious!"

"So are Vordo and Bleeker!" Joe added.

"We must get them out of here!" Frank declared. "I'll take McHugh! You two grab the others!"

Clutching the unconscious men, the boys edged their way to the cabin entrance and pushed themselves clear of the sinking aircraft. They were not too far from land and began swimming.

Joe, who was dragging Vordo along with him, looked toward the shore just as Hexton reached it. The magician stumbled ahead and disappeared into the tall grass.

"Hexton's getting away!" Joe shouted.

"We'll have to let him go," Frank replied. "We can't let Vordo and Bleeker drown."

Chet, meanwhile, was too winded to speak, as he swam doggedly on with his heavy burden. Bleeker was a dead weight. The boys had almost made it to shore when a motor launch of the Air-Sea Rescue Service sped toward them.

"We received your distress signal," one of the crewmen shouted as the boat pulled alongside. "Anybody missing?"

"No," Joe shouted back. "One man made it to shore."

Vordo and Bleeker began to recover as they were hauled aboard the boat.

"We'd better tie up these two," Frank said. "They're jewel thieves." Rope was produced and the prisoners bound.

Joe and Chet helped McHugh, who groaned and slowly got to his feet. Grief-stricken, he watched the tail of his plane disappear beneath the surface of the water in a bubbling sea of foam.

Joe began going through the prisoners' pockets. "Look!" he cried, holding out several sealskin pouches. They were crammed with jewels.

"Firsthand evidence," said Frank. "Hexton must have the rest. Now that his espionage work has been destroyed, he probably figures on living off the haul he made today."

"Let's ask these UGLI's a few questions," Joe suggested. He turned to Vordo and Bleeker. "How did you kidnap our father?"

The two men glared. "You're getting nothing out of us!" Vordo snarled.

"That's tellin' em, Vordo!" Bleeker snapped. "Too bad the mirror Hexton had you put on the road didn't work out and that Lou missed with that sandbag. We'd have been rid of these snoopers long ago! And it's a shame they have a crackerjack pilot who safely landed their plane after you loosened the fuel caps."

When the rescue ship reached shore, the prisoners were turned over to the authorities. The others proceeded to Prestwick in a car lent to McHugh by a friend. Regretfully the three boys bid good-by to the brave pilot.

"You're tops," Joe added, and Frank said. "One of the best sports I ever met!" Chet nodded.

McHugh smiled. "You're the finest lads I ever knew. Come again sometime and have a ride in my new plane."

"We'll do that," Chet answered.

After the pilot had left them, the boys went for a bite to eat. Joe expressed his frustration that Hexton had escaped.

"Where do you think he'll go?" Chet asked. "Ireland, like he said?"

Frank shook his head. "My guess is New York."

Joe's eyes lighted up. "And maybe on Flight 101! It leaves tomorrow morning."

Chet snorted, "An UGLI secret agent on Flight 101!"

"We're going to be on board, too," said Frank. "If he's there, we'll nab him."

The boys informed Inspector Clyde of their plan. They could hardly wait to take off. Next morning they watched intently as the passengers filed aboard.

"Hey!" Joe exclaimed, nudging his brother. "There's that same man we saw on our last flight to New York—the one with the dark glasses and whiskers and cane."

"Well, he can't be Hexton in disguise," Frank commented. "This man's heavier set."

"I don't see *anybody* that looks like Hexton," Chet lamented.

They observed another elderly bewhiskered man with a cast on his left leg hobble up on crutches. A steward helped him into the plane.

The boys were the last to go aboard. During the flight the boys studied the other passengers but saw nothing suspicious.

When the wheels screeched down at Westboro, Joe stretched his arms wearily. "Guess we drew a blank this time." He sighed.

At the Great Circle Airways ramp, the passengers began to debark.

"Let's keep our seats until everybody's out," Frank whispered. "Watch carefully."

The plane emptied until only the two elderly men, the three boys, and the steward were left. The man with the cast eased himself onto his crutches and started down the aisle.

Joe stiffened. "Hey! Did you see that?" he whispered excitedly. "That old man was walking on his injured leg! I'll bet he's a fake."

"I saw it too," Frank replied. He bolted out of his seat and called, "Wait a minute! We want to talk to you!"

The man stopped abruptly. Then he swung one of his crutches at Frank as the youth darted toward him. The other elderly man sprang from his seat and dealt him a blow with his cane that sent him stumbling up the aisle.

"Steward," bellowed the man with the cast, "keep these guys away from me!"

"That voice!" Joe yelled. "It's Hexton's!"

The steward was about to pounce on Frank, when Chet cried out, "This man's wanted by the police!"

Frank leaped at Hexton as the magician again swung his crutch. The young sleuth ducked and lunged forward, crashing into his opponent's midriff. As Hexton fell, his cast struck a seat and broke open. From it, a cascade of jewels spilled into the aisle. At the same moment several men poured in through the passenger door.

Among them was Kenneth Dell. "Looks as if you fellows already have things under control."

Chet picked up two sections of the cast. "It's light plastic," he said, "and looks as if it's made to come apart."

Frank yanked the magician to his feet, and whipped a wig from the man's head. Then he ripped off Hexton's false eyebrows and whiskers.

Joe whistled. "Amazing what a little disguise can do to change a man's appearance!"

"You're right!" said the other elderly man.

"We want to thank you, sir, for your help," Joe said gratefully.

"That's all right, Joe," the man replied, chuckling.

Joe! As the boys looked on in amazement, the man removed his dark glasses and a false beard.

"Dad!" the young sleuths exclaimed, overjoyed to see their father.

Then Frank whispered to him, "So you were the secret agent for SKOOL on Flight 101!"

"Yes," Mr. Hardy said quietly. His "aged" slouch was gone, and he pulled himself to his full height. "Sorry to keep my whereabouts a secret. But the job was so dangerous I couldn't risk telling anybody where I was."

"You never were in South Africa?"

"No."

Hexton was livid. "You haven't heard the last of me!" he snarled.

"Save your breath," Joe retorted. "You'll need it when the authorities begin questioning you and the other members of UGLI."

Federal agents arrived to take custody of Hexton. The boys learned that Mr. Hardy had cabled Dell to have the agents on hand because he suspected who the "injured" passenger was.

"I wanted him captured on U.S. soil," the detective said.

"Tell us, Dad," Frank asked eagerly, "how Hexton managed to spirit you away in that vanishing-man device?"

"It was quite a simple trick," Mr. Hardy explained. "The bottom of the plank I was strapped to was a highly polished mirror. After setting it in the frame, the frame was rotated so the mirror side of the plank was angled toward the audience. In this position, it reflected the roof of the enclosure, which was made of the same material as the draperies forming the rear wall. To an observer it looked as if the plank had vanished, including the subject. Meanwhile, a man of the same size and build wearing the identical clothes appeared from the wings."

"That was Lou, then," said Joe. "Bert's double. Chet, old pal, you were right about the trick."

Chet beamed modestly. "It was nothing."

"In my case," Mr. Hardy went on, "Bleeker was hiding in a secret compartment in the base of the device. When Hexton closed the curtain, he popped up and jabbed me with a needle containing a powerful drug. UGLI members always carry these hypodermics for emergencies. I passed out in seconds."

"How did you escape from the lighthouse?" Joe asked.

Fenton Hardy grinned. "I had a lucky break," he said. "Vordo and Bleeker handcuffed me to the metal railing of the spiral stairway, with my hands behind my back. Fortunately I spotted a short piece of baling wire on the floor. It was a tough job, but I managed to get the wire to stick to the heel of my shoe. Then I bent my leg back far enough so I could reach the wire with my fingers."

"And you picked the lock of your handcuffs!" Joe guessed.

"Yes," Mr. Hardy replied. "It took me hours. Then I sneaked out while Vordo and Bleeker were sleeping and borrowed their dinghy. I had almost reached the mainland when I heard their powerboat coming from the islet. So I capsized the dinghy and swam the rest of the way."

Frank grinned. "You hoped Vordo and Bleeker would find it and think you had drowned."

"Exactly," his father answered. "At least it would keep them guessing."

Mr. Hardy then described his investigations of the Great Circle stewards he suspected. "I used several disguises including a blond wig."

Chet asked him why he had tripped Ross with the cane.

"I thought maybe he had a small package of jewels in his sleeve or under his coat, and it might fall out when he fell. But I was wrong. I also slipped the note into Joe's suitcase."

"What about Mazer, the pilot of the helio-plane?" Joe inquired.

"I believe he was a victim of circumstances," Dell replied. "The authorities are going to let him off with a year's suspension of his pilot's license."

The group got out of the plane and Mr. Dell said good-by. "See you on the next case, Fenton," he called, and hurried off.

Frank and Joe fervently hoped they might be included, but first they were called upon to solve the *Mystery of the Whale Tattoo*.

"Now, fellows," Mr. Hardy said with a grin, "I suggest we call Jack Wayne and have him fly all us SKOOL boys home."

"SKOOL *boys?* What do you mean?" Chet asked.

The secret agent grinned. "I think you've all earned places in the organization as junior members!"

Match Wits with The Hardy Boys®!

Collect the Original
Hardy Boys Mystery Stories®
by Franklin W. Dixon

Celebrate 60 Years with the World's Greatest Super Sleuths!